SHIFT
RACING SERIES

In memory of
Ric Noyes
Racer, Grand Forks
Racing Hall of Fame
member, NASCAR fan
July 2024

TEAM TAYLOR

C. R. Fulton

D1547931

www.bakkenbooks.com

ISBN: 978-1-963915-04-4
Published by Bakken Books
For Worldwide Distribution
Printed in the USA

BAKKEN BOOKS

www.bakkenbooks.com

- 1 -

The roar of the engine fills my soul. I shift into high gear, doing 95 mph. A white late-model next to me surges ahead on the track.

"I don't think so!" I shout. I inch the nose of my car closer to the rail, keeping him from cutting me off. Since I was five, I've been involved in racing, and at fourteen, I've learned a few tricks.

But he hooks to the outside, and I miss the racing line. I pay for that mistake by slipping into second place through the turn. Maybe I could use a few *more* tricks.

I use the straightaway to surge up on the outside. It worked for him, so it'll work for me. My speed tops out as I reach turn three, and I brake hard. Going over 85 mph on the turns could be fatal on this short track. The car squats, the brakes suck it closer to the asphalt, but its rear end still slips sideways when I turn!

Grimacing, I feather the brake, twitching the wheel to keep the fishtail from turning into a full-blown spinout. Even with the loose rear end, I'm the one on the racing line coming into the next turn, and I aim for the apex.

Just as I thought, the move works. The other driver backs off, and I enter the straightaway with two laps remaining. I glance at the gauges. Fuel pressure and engine temps look good.

Up ahead, I'll be lapping the slowest car in the race. That's always risky. The cars getting lapped are called "back markers," and they're supposed to move over and let the faster cars pass. There are always drivers like this one, hogging the track and making passing difficult. I aim for the inside, hoping he'll see the blue flag that warns him I'm coming. But he stays right there.

"Move over!" I shout, my voice lost in the thunder of engines. I weave a little, hating to slow but having no choice.

We zip under the blue flag, but there's no

change. Then, out of the corner of my eye, I catch the white car surging forward on the outside.

"No!" It's impossible for the back marker to hear me, but his helmet still twitches my way. His eyes go wide as he realizes his mistake. Then he makes another, this one far worse. He swerves to the right, straight into the white car!

They meet in an explosion of parts and glass, pieces flying everywhere. Desperate to avoid a crash, I nail the gas and flash around the turn. I grip the wheel harder as I lap the others, zigzagging, and using every opening I can find.

Everything focuses down to a narrow tunnel as I weave through the field. It's a place I've only touched the edge of before, where my reflexes, the car, and the race condense into a singular entity. The sensation fills my chest as I surge into the far turn.

It's hard to tell which cars I'm lapping and which ones I'm racing. There's only one thing I need to know: *pass them all.* Then I'm back on the straightaway, hammering toward the finish line!

Twin flags fly. It's a combination I've never seen before—a checkered flag and a yellow caution flag. It takes a second to process. But every second counts at these breakneck speeds. Both flags are mine! I zip over the finish line and slam on the brakes. Up ahead, debris covers the asphalt.

Most of the pieces are white. Swerving, I hit a chunk of bumper with a loud thud. I wrestle 22 to the side, scanning ahead. The white car is on its roof, flames licking all around it!

Two cars spin on the oil slick while the rest of the field roars in. Everything is chaos as racers slide and smash together. The infield is abuzz with rescue personnel, but they can't reach the flaming car. There's no time to lose with flames like that, but the rescue team can't cross the track as cars still zip past.

I can, though. Ripping off my helmet and harness, I leap out of 22 and sprint past chunks of fender. The flames leap higher, and the crackle sends a shiver down my spine. The fire grows by the second as it licks up the oily fuel slick below the car.

"Hey!" I shout, desperate for the driver to respond. "*Hey!*"

I skid on my knees, shielding my face with one arm. The fire's so hot! What I see makes my stomach turn. The driver's arms dangle toward the track as he sags against his harness. *He's not conscious.*

Rescuers pour onto the field, but each second

could mean life or death in the merciless heat. If the driver's breathing, its searing hot air. I dive into the flames. My suit is fire retardant, and I've got to trust it. It's impossible to breathe with the fire consuming all the oxygen!

His harness buckle burns my fingers even through my gloves. With a pop, the harness opens, and the driver slumps to the roof. I grab his wrist and pull for all I'm worth. Backing through the blaze, I take a full breath as more hands join mine, pulling the driver free.

A deep coughing fit grips me, making me double over as I try to clear the acrid smoke from my lungs. Just then I notice the other driver isn't coughing. *Is he even breathing?* Emergency workers surround him, rolling him onto a stretcher. I cover my face, praying he'll make it.

Somebody grabs me, and I lash out, my adrenaline surging.

"Take it easy. I won't hurt you," an EMT says, pulling back the thin hood I wear under my helmet. "You've got a burn."

At his words, my neck pulses with pain. I grimace as he presses a cool cloth over it.

"Hold this for a minute."

I lift my hand but end up staring at my glove. It's as black as sin and bubbled from the heat.

"Take them off, so I can see your hands," the EMT says.

I pull them off, watching as if they belong to someone else. The tip of my pointer finger is an angry red from when I forced the harness to release.

"I figured it would be way worse," the EMT says. "What brand are those gloves? I'm impressed."

I don't respond. Between my burning lungs and the tension in my chest as I watch them administer CPR to the driver, it's all I can do to remain standing.

The racer flinches and coughs. The crowd of rescuers goes wild, working faster, but I fall to my knees.

"Thank you," I whisper.

"Whoa, we better get you to the ambulance." The EMT holds my arm, steadying me.

"No, I'm fine. I thought I was too late; that's all."

"You're the one who pulled him out?"

I nod, exhaustion setting in. Sitting down might be a good idea.

"But you're just a kid," the man says.

I shrug, trying not to take it as an insult. "I'm fourteen."

Mom appears, her face a mask of worry. "Logan!"

"I'm fine, Mom, honest."

"This is your son?" the EMT asks.

She nods, wrapping me in a hug, then takes over holding the cloth. "I had hoped that moving here would keep you safe."

The EMT pours a bottle of water over my hand, which eases the searing heat in my fingertip for a second. "Well, he's a hero!"

- 2 -

By the time the medical team clears me, with only minor burns, the announcer pulls me forward.

"Folks," he says, his voice reverberating through the stands, "Logan Reed is our winner for stock late models today. But there's another win that happened here tonight. Jimmy Bella is still alive thanks to this young man's courage. Logan, tell us about it."

Still out of sorts, I shrug. "It was a tight race. Jimmy's a skilled driver, but he got caught in a tight place. I hope he's back to racing soon."

As the crowd goes wild, I realize I forgot to thank my sponsor, Taylor Racing! That's priority number one in the winner's circle. My face reddens as I turn to John. His expression is hard to see under his blue baseball cap and the glaring track lights.

"I'm so sorry! I–"

"Nope." He holds up a hand. "Don't say a word. Team Taylor is honored to have you. Let's take you back to the pits. You must be tired."

I let out a breath, filled with thankfulness just to be alive. Then I see our car. Its black, red, and white paint is nicked up, and the 22 on its side reminds me of Bobby. He used to be John's main racer, but he walked off the team with his brother, Billy. That I got to drive this car tonight is so huge, I think my knees might buckle.

As they clear the track for the next race, I pick my helmet off the ground and hop in. Moments later, it's hard to believe I'm pulling up to the huge Team Taylor trailer, easily the nicest in the pits.

"Don't mess up, Logan," I mutter to myself. Keeping the team in the winner's circle is our top priority. And that means holding up under the massive pressure of racing and school combined.

The engine's purr is like my heartbeat. 77 still bears the scars from its last race, but it's a super late model, a true race car. I'm glad for the win in 22, but 77 is my favorite by far.

I'm desperate to race, but without a proper mechanic, the cars aren't fit for it.

"Put it in gear!" My crew chief, Slate Emory, stands up from under 77, dusting off his hands. He has a smear of grease in his blond hair.

I nod, my right hand on the shifter. "Come on, boy," I whisper. "You've got to work!"

It's our sixth try today. I shift into low gear and let the clutch out slowly.

Tick. Tick. Pop. Whir.

"Shut it off, Logan!" Slate shouts over the awful clatter.

In the complete silence that follows, I lean my head back against the seat.

Slate's massive forearms settle on the windowsill, his usual smile gone. "We need a real mechanic. *Bad.*"

I nod. Team Taylor lost a mechanic and a driver not too long ago, and it's painfully obvious that Slate and I won't cut it.

"Did you call that guy?" I ask, running a hand through my shaggy hair.

Slate hangs his head. "His back surgery went wrong. The doc told him no more engines. *Ever.*"

I sigh. When Billy walked off the team, I was

glad to see him go. But we're in a pinch now. It's impossible to race cars if they don't run. And 77's transmission needs a touch of true genius.

"I've put ads on social media, professional racing sites . . . everything. The only people who responded are backyard mechanics unfamiliar with racing specs."

"Well, at least we can race the other cars," I say, looking at 22.

Slate laughs. "The stock car needs a timing belt. The legend might take one more race before it needs a serious tune-up, and the mini cup needs a rear-end adjustment."

I rub my forehead, then my phone goes off. It's an alarm I'd set last week to study for my math exam.

"Slate, can you run me home? I'll never set foot on the track again if I don't ace my schoolwork."

"Yeah. You never will if we don't find a mechanic either."

I don't know Slate that well yet, but it's unusual to see him down. Can't say I blame him. John Taylor's a millionaire, but he doesn't own a race team for fun. He's out to win, and it's Slate's job to make it happen. Slate is the mastermind behind us all. He's what makes this team tick. It's a lot of weight on his shoulders. I pull myself out of 77's window and pat its hood. It's the fastest car I've ever driven. "Don't worry, we'll get you going again."

Slate gives me a look. "You're talking to them now?"

I shrug. "Seventy-seven is special. I can feel it."

Slate shakes the tension from his shoulders. "Yeah, it's really special sitting there. Broken."

"I guess you and I don't quite make a team, do we?"

"I'll tell you one thing. You and I being on the same page and going after the same dreams will make or break Team Taylor. I spent a year trying to cram knowledge into Bobby's head, but it was too full already. I succeed when you do, and you succeed when I do. That's how it is with a crew chief and driver."

I nod. Winning is definitely my goal.

"It doesn't look that way at the smaller tracks where races are short and the field is full of cowboys with cars. But John's never been content here. He's been waiting for a driver who can take this team higher. A lot higher."

"Yes, sir," I say, a thrill streaking up from my toes. "You might have to wait for a mechanic."

We get in Slate's big white Dodge truck. The engine's rumble is a soothing rhythm. "We may end up training someone," he says, "which will set our racing schedule way back."

I shake my head. "That will take forever, though. Are you sure we can't find someone with some real experience?"

"I still have some feelers out with local mechanics, but at the end of the day we gotta do what we gotta do. If that means doing it the hard way and training in a new guy, that's what we'll do. Unless you want to give up on our dreams?"

He's got a point there.

- 3 -

Mom and I order a new racing suit and gloves, since mine got sizzled. I can't wait to gear up in the fresh colors, which match Team Taylor's.

"Oh, wait! Can you order that too?" I ask, pointing to an ad on the screen.

"Are you starting a new sport?" she asks.

"It's not for me . . . " I say.

"Ah, it wouldn't be for some young lady, would it?"

I wish I could squash the teasing light in her eyes. The problem is, she's right.

Later, I'm in my bedroom, deep inside the confusing world of Algebra One. I wonder if algebra could help me plot a course through school where

I'll never bump into Gabe, who hates my guts. I'm still studying quadratics and writing out long equations when my phone rings. It's Slate.

A shiver rushes down my spine. I hope it's good news. "Yeah?"

"I found a guy! He's really young, near your age, but he's brilliant. It only took him two minutes to figure out where we went wrong with Seventy-seven's transmission!" The relief in Slate's voice is clear. "You've got to meet him! I'll pick you up in twenty minutes."

"Sure," I say, but I think he's already hung up. The guy must be good for Slate to be this excited. There's no way I can hope to get back to 2 (4-y)-3 (y+3) = -11 with this news. I run down the hall to tell Mom.

"Did you finish your homework?" she asks before I can get a word out.

"Yes, of course. I was doing some extra."

I can't believe those words just came out of my mouth. Considering my first eight years of school consisted of . . . well, it was cheating, plain and simple. I never realized how difficult it would be to get good grades on my own. And I'm not anywhere near good enough. I'm still teetering on the line where Mom is threatening to pull me from the racing team. But tutoring and extra study haven't killed me—*yet.*

"Alright, you can go, but I want you home by ten."

"Sweet." I kiss her cheek, then grab a slice of pizza and a doughnut from the fridge and run toward the road.

Still, the nagging questions about why we moved here eat at me. Mom's lack of response makes it easier to forget, but I vow to figure it out someday. This place is growing on me, though. With the glittering river behind the house, there's always a hint of salt water in the air. We can't be more than two miles from the Atlantic Ocean. Two days ago, I saw a dolphin swimming up the river from my bedroom window! All there was in Iowa was corn.

Slate's shiny truck pulls up, and we start the familiar ride to John's house. It's a mansion, set far back from the road, but the only part I'm interested in is the shop. That's where my heartbeat is, 77.

Slate can't contain his excitement. "He's got twice as much raw talent as Billy ever did. This kid could really set us apart from the rest. He even knows how to pull more horsepower from the super."

I try to imagine 77 with more horsepower.

"Sounds perfect. Did he sign a contract with Taylor yet?"

"It might take a bit for John to write something for him since he's been at the shop all afternoon."

As we pull in, I'm bursting with excitement. 77 will be ready to go soon! "When will he be able to start?"

"We haven't gotten that far yet."

I hop out but try to look cool by not showing the intense excitement brewing inside. It's a weird feeling, knowing I'll probably be spending hours of my life with a person I've yet to meet.

I step into the relative dimness of the shop and

let my eyes adjust. Soft voices reach me from the back of the spacious area. I run my fingers over 77 as I pass, Slate leading the way.

"Logan, I'd like to introduce you to . . . "

I stop in my tracks, my mouth hanging open in horror. "Gabe?"

His name sounds like a dirty word in my mouth. *Why does it have to be him?*

– 4 –

We face each other. Archenemies. His familiar scowl makes my muscles tense.

"Naw, man!" Gabe says, shaking his head while one hand chops the air.

Slate's eyes go wide. "Um . . . Do you two know each other?"

Gabe and I glare at each other like wolves, neither willing to back off but unable to avoid each other either.

"I ain't fixing *his* cars," Gabe replies, crossing his arms.

"Well, the cars belong to me, actually," John says, his eyes like ping-pong balls.

"Which one does *he* drive?" Gabe asks, pointing at me. His gaze is full of fire, as usual.

"All of them," Slate replies, stepping between us. "Logan is our only driver. He's a stellar one too. Got quite a track record."

Slate's words shore up the bruised sensation in my gut. Gabe being here feels so wrong, as if something sacred has been thrown into the street.

Gabe shakes his head. "Count me out." He turns to John. "Can I get a ride home now?"

"Um . . . " John stutters, but Slate frowns at John. The look that passes between them shows how long they've worked together. "Sure thing, Gabe. You want to take the Ferrari?"

Gabe's jaw drops. "You . . . you have a Ferrari?" He follows John out.

When it's just Slate and me, he gives me a look. "Care to explain what just happened?"

"You saw it. He hates me," I say with a shrug, acting as if it doesn't matter.

"Why?"

I lean on 22 and cross my arms. "Well . . . on my first day here . . . "

When I finish relating the story, Slate rubs his forehead. "What are the chances?"

"Pretty high, apparently. How good can he be?

He's just a kid."

Slate's eyebrows go up. "I could say the same for you! In fact, he's a year older than you."

My face goes red. "You're right. But mechanics is a deep field, and it just doesn't . . . " My words trail off. He's right. I'm a fourteen-year-old doing 130 mph on asphalt. "Point taken."

"The question is, how do we fix it? We need him." Slate's bright blue eyes bore into mine.

I raise my hands in the air. "If there's one thing I'm sure of, it's that I can't change Gabe's mind."

"*Can't* is a dangerous thought."

"Fine. Here's the truth. I'm not sure I *want* to," I say, jutting out my chin.

"What? Is your brain functioning? You're willing to let some petty dislike stop your entire racing career? If so, I'll tell John you're not cut from the same cloth as we are."

"No . . . No . . . It's just . . . " The flame of anger against Gabe runs so deep I can't see past it. But if I want to race, I'll have to. "You got any ideas?"

"Just one. You apologize for being a thorn in his side and beg him to come back." Slate pins me with a look.

I frown, waving a hand in dismissal, but he's serious. The problem is, Gabe has hated me from the moment we met, and I've gotten used to protecting myself, but Slate isn't giving up.

"How bad do you want it, Logan? Let's see what you're made of."

I sigh, looking out the garage door at the brilliant sunset. Racing would be simpler without people. Cars are so honest.

"I've scraped the bottom of the barrel, Logan. Our next step is to take 77 to some street mechanic and hope he gets our *very* different specs just right for the track. You and I know the disaster that would be.

"Gabe has worked at his uncle's shop since he was seven. He knows engines backward and forward. Plus, his uncle's been itching to get into racing. He even bought a 'race car' last year. Gabe has taken on the job of fixing that piece of junk. It's actually worth driving now since he worked on it. He's more than capable. Plus, he knows the rules on all these cars. I quizzed him."

Slate leans back, his gaze still fixed on me, leaving me no way out. "That car he fixed for his uncle? Everything he's done to it is astonishing. It blew my mind. Legit."

Slate lets those words hang there. I sigh again. "I still don't see any way to change Gabe's mind."

"Oh, he wants out. Leaving the small shop for the world of high-class racecars is his dream. He got a taste of it here today. You should've seen his eyes light up when we showed him around. It's up to you to fix this, Logan. Our team is riding on your shoulders."

"Great. Just great. What's the plan?" I ask.

"You apologize and sort out your differences. Remember, this isn't just your dream; it's Gabe's too."

"Ugh."

- 5 -

By morning, a plan *slightly* different from Slate's forms in my mind. I'm two minutes late and in grave danger of missing the bus. Mrs. Brown waits for no man. Still, I careen into the garage, grab what I need, and sprint down the long drive. Sweat rolls off my shoulder blades as I watch the bus lurch into gear to pull away.

"Mrs. Brown!" I shout, waving frantically. "Wait!"

She's already closing the door! My legs churn, and I jam my hand into the narrowing gap.

"Well, you made it, Mr. Reed." She doesn't sound pleased as she lets me in.

"Whew!" I take a second to catch my breath before getting on. I won't let Gabe think last night's incident affected my attendance or intimidated me. I'll use every trick to make this work.

As the bus heads toward school, I consider all the ways my plan could go wrong. *Rage.* That's definitely a possibility. *Scoffing.* I've seen that one from him before. Seeing this *work* is the most difficult thing. I finger the chrome wrench in my bag. It's got a scuff at one end, but maybe it will be the key to fixing things.

I don't see Gabe until third period. I've gotten pretty good at avoiding him. That's what I plan to do today. Waiting until lunch, when I'll have a little time, is my only hope.

The day creeps by. I try to take notes during class but I'm extra distracted today. Piper, the prettiest tutor in the world, will have to help me catch up. I remind myself to text her a video I found about a nearby skateboard competition next month.

When the bell finally rings, it sends a shot of adrenaline to my fingertips. It's time for lunch.

I don't bother getting a tray. There won't be time for that today. Besides, my stomach is rolling. My gaze locks on Gabe with his posse of friends sitting at their usual table. *Step one: divide. Step two:*

conquer. I stride up to him from behind, and his buddies heckle me right away.

Gabe shifts, looking over his shoulder. He shakes his head and then turns back around.

"Gabe."

He doesn't respond. I stand there, boring holes into the back of his neck with my eyes.

"Get lost," he growls.

"Not gonna happen," I reply.

Two boys across the table stand up, threatening. I don't bat an eye. "This is between me and him."

To my surprise, they sit back down.

Gabe launches to his feet, whipping around until his nose is only an inch from mine. "You got a hearing problem? I said, get lost!"

There's the rage part. I hold my ground, leaning in closer, sticking to my plan. "Two minutes. That's all."

We glare at each other. His jaw flexes, but he doesn't shove me away.

"One minute, tops."

I keep glaring, even though my legs feel like jelly.

"In the hall." I stalk away without glancing back. Now for the tricky part . . .

Once we're out in the hall, he crosses his arms. "Time is ticking."

I pull out the wrench and hold it between us.

"What's that for?" he asks, sneering. "Slate said you can't fix cars." There's the scoffing part.

I bite back a million retorts. *Focus, Logan. Your entire career is on the line.*

"It's the 'wrench of peace.' John Taylor has everything you need—the cars, the experience, the chance to carve out your own name in the world of top-class racing. The day I signed a contract with him, everything changed. You deserve the same chance." I almost choke on those words, but it's as close as I can come to following Slate's advice.

Heartbeats pass like sludge.

He reaches out and snatches the wrench from my hand. Without a word, he turns and walks away. I stand there, staring at my empty palm. *What on earth does this mean? Will he join Team Taylor? Did I just ruin everything?*

Scowling, I turn and walk away, uncaring if the hall monitor catches me. There's no way I'm setting foot in that cafeteria again today, not with so much tension in the air.

My next three classes are nothing but a blur. Then after the last bell, I step into room 202. I stop near the door, remembering how much I hated that room on my first day. Now, tutoring is my favorite part of school. Piper walks up, raking her fingers through her long brown hair, her smile lighting up the hallway.

"Ready for something new?"

If it's from you, yes, I think, but I play it cool and shrug. "Sure."

We sit at the end of the room. "I've been reading about a new way to remember things," Piper says, her brown eyes shining. "It's called spatial learning."

"Does that mean I'll get to race a spaceship?" I quip, enjoying how other parts of my life disappear when I'm near her.

She rolls her eyes. "No, humans remember the best by using areas or space. Here, close your eyes." I do, wondering what she's up to. "How many windows does your house have?"

"I thought we were doing schoolwork." Pestering Piper is one of my favorite things. This thought shocks me so much that I open my eyes. Racing's been my one and only. I'm unsure how to handle this new revelation.

She punches my arm. "Come on, Logan! Close your eyes and picture how many."

I close my eyes, if only to escape my thoughts

combined with how pretty she is. I answer immediately. "Thirty-two."

"Thirty-two windows? How big is your house?
Mine only has eighteen. Wait, how did you do that
so fast?"

I open my eyes. She's just as pretty as she was
seconds earlier. "It's a big house. I didn't need to
see anything. My parents are getting new windows
installed, so I already knew the number."

"Cheater," she says with a grin.

The word takes me back. I *was* a cheater, and I
have to make things right, so I close my eyes again.
"Okay, give me another."

"Fine. How about the stoplights between school
and your house?"

In my mind I'm in 77 on the open road. I slam
my foot on the classroom floor as if I'm in the car,
then I shift, making engine sounds. I get home
pretty fast—in my head. "Seven."

Piper giggles. "See? You had that information
stored somewhere in your brain. Spatial. See?
Here's how we can use it in school. What's your
favorite place?"

"My racecar," I say without hesitation, thankful
for the balance the words bring.

"That's your favorite place on the entire planet?"

I nod. *Or maybe right here next to you.* I clench my jaw to keep that thought inside. Such thoughts are dangerous. They want to leap out and ruin everything.

"Oh yeah, I've been meaning to ask . . . You said you know John Taylor?"

"Yep. I race for him."

"As in, like . . . " She stumbles for words, which only boosts her cuteness. "*Real* racecars?"

I give her a cheeky grin. "Of course. Let me show you." I pull out my phone and show her 77.

"Wow."

"That's exactly what I was hoping you'd say."

She laughs. "Okay. Back to spatial learning. You're in your car. Now you start leaving facts inside it. Like this one: Germany invaded Poland on September 1, 1939. That goes on the door handle. Then on the steering wheel you might put September 2, 1945, the date World War Two ended."

I make a horrified face. "I can't do that to 77. Maybe I should use a different space."

"Of course! As long as you know it well."

As usual, the hour flies by. When Piper gathers her things, a deep sigh escapes me.

"You alright? We didn't break your brain today, did we?" she asks, stepping into the empty hallway.

"Naw. It's just . . . Have you ever had to do something really hard to reach a goal?"

From the look in her eyes, I know she's not going to give me a fluffy answer. "Yeah. This is it."

My head jerks in response. "Talking to me?"

"Well, not you specifically." She turns around, her arms spread wide. "Room 202 was the most terrifying thing."

My face must betray my disbelief.

"No, really, it's true. I was so shy I couldn't look anybody in the eye, much less talk to them."

"For real?" Her story makes me forget my own.

"I was failing everything, math most of all. Then Mrs. Morgan told me I had to come here or they would send me to special classes. For two weeks I sat in my cocoon of terror, all by myself. Finally, she took me aside and told me something that changed my life." Piper goes quiet for so long I can't stand it.

"Well, what was it?"

She looks at me until I'm sure she's gazing straight into my soul. Then her mouth softens into a shadow of a smile. "I've never told anyone this before."

Heat flushes up my neck, but I don't look away.

"Mrs. Morgan said I was the proudest person she'd ever met."

"*What?*" I reply. I'd expected anything else.

Piper nods. "It shocked me too. I'd always thought of myself as the worst human ever. That no one cared about me. Nobody at home does, at least." She rolls her eyes, I don't think she meant to let that slip. "She said pride is thinking you're the best *or* the worst. At its core, it's just thinking about *you*. People who only think about themselves live in a small world." Piper's smile grows wistful, even fond. "I'm so glad she did."

"Why?" I ask, furious at Mrs. Morgan.

"Because she was *right*. I was so wrapped up in myself that I couldn't even speak. The next day it took me fifty-nine minutes to work up the courage to ask her how to fix it." Piper laughs at herself.

"I can't imagine you being that shy."

"Right? Mrs. Morgan said the first step was to notice who I was thinking about. Second, she said even a smile can be a way to help someone else. It was tough at first. But when someone smiled back at me, something broke open inside. It felt fantastic because for once I wasn't the center of my universe."

Piper looks over her shoulder, making sure no one else heard. A warm feeling fills my chest. *A secret.* Just between us.

"So, what were you thinking before my way-too-much-info dump?" she asks, raising one eyebrow.

"No, it wasn't too much. You're an amazing person." Those words make my knees feel weak, so I rush into my story.

Her mouth hangs open as I describe the whole thing. Tutoring takes up almost all our time, and I wish we got more moments like this.

"I'm still getting over the fact that you race real cars. But what did he mean by taking the 'wrench of peace'?"

"That's what I'd like to know!"

She crosses her arms, then looks up at the ceiling. "Gabe and I . . . We have . . . sort of . . . a history."

I feel like a boulder the size of Colorado just settled on my shoulders. "A history?"

I hope my face isn't as pale as it feels. Piper sighs, shifting her backpack.

"He asked me out. More times than one. But I need to concentrate on school, so I said no. He didn't take it very well."

It's everything I can do to remain standing. I

blink, struggling to assimilate what she just said. *Gabe likes her.* That's why he got so upset when he saw me staring on the first day of school. Plus, his buddy Marco knew it too. A million things mix in my mind. Yet another reason for Gabe's intense dislike of me.

I blink, realizing that Piper would say the same to me if I asked her. I'd have more air in my lungs if Slate had run over me with the semi-truck.

She glances at her phone. "Oh no! I'm late for the bus! I've got to run. Bye!" she takes off down the hall, her long hair rippling behind her. Then she turns. "Logan Reed, I'm glad you're my friend!"

I watch her go, trying not to puke. Gabe must know she's tutoring me. Now I'm the rich kid who took the girl he wanted. The only problem is, I don't actually have the girl.

Friend. The word stings in my ears.

– 6 –

A few hours later, Mom drops me off at John's shop after a fruitless homework session during which my brain circled like a B-17 bomber over my problems. I inhale the perfect scent of fuel, oil, and tires. I spot a pair of legs sticking out from under 77, a rolling creeper beneath them.

"Hey, Slate," I say. That's about everything I've prepared in my speech to explain how I failed. The creeper rolls out. Gabe Silva stares up at me.

As I try to regain my composure, I realize Gabe's eyes lack their normal flicker of anger.

"Got the tranny fixed," he says as if nothing's weird.

So, that's the deal. He'll act like everything is cool.

No arguments, no hatred. That's fine by—

"Don't expect me to be at your beck and call," he snarls as he stands up.

Never mind. I square my shoulders. "Trust me, if I had a choice, you wouldn't be here."

I regret the words as soon as they're out, even though they're true. The past few hours had fueled my anger toward Gabe. Just knowing he likes Piper is enough to make my blood boil. It's a pretty sorry situation, considering how excited Piper is to be my friend. *Friend.* That's all. Gabe and I face the same challenge.

His mouth turns down, and he steps toward me, clenching his fists.

Movement catches my eye. Slate strides up. "Boys, this is a professional race team. Leave the personal *junk* at home. We expect you to act like you work here because you do." He turns to Gabe. "Is it ready to test?"

"Yes, sir." He looks down. At least Slate can make him back off.

"Logan, take a ride down the drive. If everything checks out, we'll head to the speedway to heat it up real good."

Now that's something I *can* do. I hop through

the window and settle into the seat. It hugs my sides and legs, fitting like a glove. I push the button on the dash. The engine cranks, and I hold my breath as I shift into low.

I catch Slate's eye. We've done this enough times to feel the stress.

"Here goes," I whisper, hesitating.

"I said I fixed it," Gabe insists, though I can only see his lips move. His eyes are even darker than normal.

Slate nods at me, so I let out the clutch. 77 rolls forward, the tranny completely silent. Slate slaps Gabe's back. "Now we're in business!"

But I'm out of earshot because 77's eating up the distance. I feel alive again now that 77 is running, even though I can't go fast on the long driveway.

As I thunder back into the shop, Slate and Gabe are lowering the semi-trailer's ramp. Gabe's face is full of awe as he takes in the mobile shop. I grin. He can't resist this opportunity any more than I could. The question is, do I want him to stay?

As the three of us push 77 into the trailer, I know the answer is "yes." Racing is worth the discomfort of Gabe's presence.

"Boys, let's see what we've got."

I've never ridden in the semi before, but there are two bunk beds in the back. Since I get in first, I take the lower bunk. I'd like to sprawl out on it, but Gabe has me nervous, so I perch on its edge. He takes the passenger seat, but the air still seems to crackle around him.

Slate shifts through the semi's gears, and we ride to Carteret in complete silence. He backs the big trailer up to the pits and then turns to us. "Your icy silence could freeze the Bahamas. I'm out of here."

When he hops out, Gabe turns, pinning me with a glare. "*Never* say a word to the boys about me being here. Just because we work together doesn't mean we know each other in school. I'm no rich kid's lackey."

His words hit me like a punch in the chest. Here's the real root of the problem: he hates me because of the money my parents have. Maybe he doesn't know I ride a bike to the track.

But he's out of the truck before I can reply. I sigh, the scent of the track filling my lungs. It will be worth it. My hands tremble with excitement as I settle the steering wheel in place.

"The moment of truth," Slate says, slapping the roof.

I try not to hold my breath as I take the track. It's just the car and me, with no hindrances. The massive engine roars, but the tranny stays quiet. I enter that incredible place where it seems like 77 and I are one.

After lap five, everything is smooth. Still, Slate waves me in on the next lap. 77's chrome steering wheel glints in the lights as I pull to a stop in the pits. The moment sears itself into my brain. Gabe's attitude doesn't matter; this is my calling.

Slate and Gabe shout over the engine noise. I can't make out what they're saying. Slate makes a motion at me as if he's turning off a key. I reach up and hit the kill switch as Gabe disappears under 77.

Then all I hear are frogs and crickets in the warm air. Slate's eyes gleam. "Gabe's got an idea for the fuel pressure. We'll see what it does to the performance."

A few minutes later, I'm cruising around the track again. In turn two I feather the gas, and 77 lunges forward.

"Whoa!" Whatever Gabe did, it definitely gave 77 a huge power boost. I keep my eye on the fuel pressure gauge, knowing Slate will want a full report.

I settle my hands into a firm grip on the wheel, determined to make this my fastest lap on a 4/10-

mile track ever. Handling the turns leaves me no time to think. There's only the feel of the tires slipping and of the g-force pulling me to the outside.

Slate slams down the stopwatch, then punches the air as I whip past. A wide grin presses my cheeks against my helmet. I cruise into the pits to find Slate still leaping up and down, pumping his fist like he's dealing out uppercuts. Gabe stands beside him, his arms crossed, scowling. But deep inside me a fire smolders. I hate the way Gabe judges me. I pull myself out of the car, full of conflicting passions. Part of me loves the infinite possibilities of racing. Another part hates that I need Gabe to be there.

"Hooah!" Slate slaps my shoulder so hard I nearly fall. "Ten point one seconds!" Then he turns to Gabe. "What did you do?"

He shrugs, "The car's got a lot more to give. It would excel on a longer track. That's what it's made for. I have a few more tweaks in mind."

Slate shakes out his hands. "Boys, let's get loaded, then I'll take you home; it's on the way. Tonight's times will make John a very happy man."

Soon, we're back in the semi, but the frosty silence between Gabe and I continues. I retreat into the memory of how 77 handled and how it held to the track, my mind surging between wanting to box Gabe and just being glad he isn't boxing me.

Slate cranks the enormous steering wheel, and we turn onto my road. He brakes a long time before we reach my driveway. I'm about to correct him, but Gabe unclips his seatbelt.

I look out. Beyond a wild sprawl of bushes, security lights reveal a group of small mobile homes. Many sag in the center, with broken windows covered in plastic.

"See you," Slate says. Gabe nods but refuses to look back as he hops out. After he slams the door, Slate motions me up to the passenger seat. He releases the air brake, but he doesn't pull away. "Now you know why *the rich kid* bothers him."

"But it's not my fault. I don't judge him by where he lives or how much he has."

"There's the rub." Slate nods, shifting into first. "He can't stand having to look up."

"But I'm not higher than he is!" I lean back in the seat. Did Gabe know it was me who moved in nearby when we first met? Was I automatically disqualified because of my address?

"Doesn't matter much when that's the way *he*

thinks it is. Best you can do is prove it. He'll have to get over things."

"Easier said than done," I reply, thinking of Piper.

Slate checks his side mirrors, downshifting to a stop at my driveway. "Now I'm a bus driver," he mutters. "We're gonna have to do something different here. I can't spend half the day playing chauffeur." Then he looks at me. "Ten point one seconds! John is going to be thrilled!"

That makes me grin. "Yeah, it felt great."

I hop out into the dark and watch the beautiful yellow truck and trailer pull away. Not even Gabe can dampen the wild joy inside me. I shout for all I'm worth, the sound echoing over the brackish river. A flock of birds takes off from the reeds in response to my roar.

- 7 -

The next day, Mom drops me off at the shop, but the second I step inside, I know something's wrong. The air feels heavy. Nobody's inside. I can't remember a time when Slate wasn't here.

"Hello?" I call, but my voice echoes into nothing.

Tiptoeing along, I catch a flash of blue and red lights reflecting on the chrome. My heartbeat picks up as I rush forward. Police cars surround John's house! My shoes peel out as I run for the back door. I arrive breathless near the group of officers.

Slate's there, his expression serious. I ease up to him, eyeing the officers as they talk with John. His face is pale as he answers their questions.

"What happened?" I whisper to Slate.

He frowns, leaning closer. "The Ferrari was stolen last night."

"Sophia?" I cry.

"Shh," he hisses.

I flinch as the officers look our way.

"Yes, Sophia. The car is replaceable; insurance will cover the theft. Problem is, John had a very important laptop in Sophia. Now, there's a chance that the thief hasn't found it, since John stores it in a secret compartment under the back seat, but he's still really worried about the personal information on his laptop being compromised. The thieves could do a lot of financial damage to him with what's on there."

I turn, looking at the open garage door. The empty spot looks like a tomb.

"Any idea who would do this?" an officer asks John.

My heart responds immediately: *Gabe Sliva!* His eyes gleamed when he heard about Sophia. Plus, he rode in Sophia just two nights ago, and that means he knows where John parks her.

"No. None at all." John crosses his arms. "The real question is, how did they start it? I just had a code to start button installed, and I change the number every week!"

I cringe at his tone. I've never heard him so distressed. But it fits my theory exactly. Gabe watched him start Sophia, so he would have the current start code. Wouldn't a car like that solve all of his family's money issues?

First, I'll need some clues to follow. A mass of wires hangs from a box on the garage wall. I step closer, studying them. The thief broke the gray plastic covering, but I can still read the word "security" printed there. Then the thief cut some wires and twisted them onto others.

The shiny copper wires make me think of Gabe knowing engines forward and backward. Wiring is a must for any mechanic, so I bet this would be easy for someone like Gabe.

I rush over to the group of police officers, ready to unload my theory.

"And who is this?" A tall police officer points at me, and I flinch.

"I . . . I'm Logan Reed, Team Taylor's driver."

He flips through a list on his clipboard. "You're on our list of suspects."

"What?" I cry.

John turns toward us. "Don't worry, Logan. It's

procedure for them to look at everyone who's familiar with the property."

Another officer pulls John aside, leaving me to face the intimidating man who is staring me down. "I'll need to ask you a few questions."

It seems like all the air has left earth. "I . . . " I gasp, getting a full breath. "Okay."

"I'm Officer Wells. Where were you last night?" His pen is poised over a notepad. It makes the situation feel like a test, which only adds to my frayed nerves.

"Um . . . Well . . . I was home."

"Can anyone verify that?"

The tension eases in my shoulders. "Of course. My mom was there since five o'clock."

He frowns, then asks for her number. I wonder if Gabe has an alibi . . .

- 8 -

By third period, I can't think of anything except my growing suspicion that Gabe stole Sophia. But why would he do it? He's going to ruin both of our dreams over some money! I clench my fists, rage overflowing. The halls are crowded, but I navigate through. I don't know what to do. If I catch Gabe red-handed, I can prove to John that he's no good, but then Team Taylor would still need a mechanic. Maybe I can convince Gabe to return the car and the laptop, and John will have some mercy, as unlikely as that seems.

Then I see Gabe ahead as he veers into the men's room. Containing myself is next to impossible. How could he do this to John and Slate? After everything they offered to him—being part of the team and working on super late models—it's an opportunity like no other, and Gabe is just going to throw it away!

When I reach the door, Gabe's stepping out. And just like he promised, he ignores me. *Don't act like I know you in school.*

Why? Because I might figure out what he's been up to! He and his little clique have some darker secrets than I imagined.

He turns, the crowd swallowing him. I consider confronting him, but my thoughts are too chaotic to make a decision, and I don't have any solid evidence. I shift my weight back and forth as I stand in front of the bathroom door. Then I hear a muffled voice . . .

"With that 6.5-liter V-12, yeah, it'll be fast."

I plaster my ear to the wood, not caring about the looks I receive. That's Sophia's engine!

"But who's gonna drive? Max is out. He broke his leg last week."

My thoughts clash. *Wait, are they planning to road race Sophia? Maybe that's how Gabe managed to fix up a race car when he's only fourteen!*

"Excuse me," another kid says, pushing past

me through the door. I glimpse an older boy with a phone held to his ear standing near the sink. He looks like a senior and has tattoos on both forearms.

If I let this slender thread of a clue slip away, I might never find another. Before I lose my nerve, I enter the restroom.

The senior tucks the phone into his back pocket as the other kid rushes out. I don't step up to the sink; I just cross my arms.

"Seven hundred and eighty-nine horse is a fast engine." My stomach rolls. This guy's a rough character, the kind of kid I've always veered far away from. If I play this wrong, it won't be pretty. But I have to find Sophia!

He hisses, shaking his head. "Whatever you heard, forget about it."

I shrug as if I couldn't care less. "It's not the fastest engine I've ever raced." I might throw up, but I press on, determined to expose Gabe. "But a GTS is a decent car."

He frowns at me, crossing his arms. "You race?"

I nod. "Yeah, supers on an asphalt track. But I'm looking for something different." I glance away, so he won't see my nerves. "Something. . . riskier."

My words hang in between us.

"Might have something for you," he says.

I flinch, covering it by running a hand through my hair. "When? Where?"

"Tonight. Smith's airfield. Eight o'clock sharp." He pushes past me out the door.

I collapse against the sink, my eyes sliding shut. I sure hope it's Sophia. If not, I'm in over my head. Way over.

- 9 -

I stomp into the shop with only hours until the meet at the airfield. My blood boils when I see Gabe standing there with Slate. He's got a lot of guts to show up here.

Slate looks down at his clipboard. "So, you can fix the wiring issue on the legend car and tune up the stock car today."

"Sure thing, boss," Gabe says, flipping a wrench in his hand. He turns, catching sight of me, and frowns. We stare each other down.

The air between us seems electrified. He grabs another tool and turns to the engine.

"Logan, step into the office. We've got a few things to cover," Slate says, reaching for the door.

"You bet we do," I mutter, following him. I've always admired Slate, but now I wonder how he's missing so many clues that point to Gabe.

"You okay?" he asks as we sit down in the quiet office.

"It's just . . . Can't you see it was Gabe who took Sophia?" I whisper, leaning forward.

"Gabe?" Slate sits back in his chair as if the idea's new to him. "No, it wasn't him."

"What makes you so sure?" I ask, inching my chair closer.

He sighs. "Just trust me. John almost had a nervous breakdown last night about that laptop, and if there was any evidence that it was Gabe he would have the police all over it."

I cross my arms, more determined than ever to help John. "But Gabe could have easily chopped those garage alarm wires. Look what he's doing right now! Plus, he watched John start Sophia before she was stolen. He knew the code."

Slate shakes his head. "Just let it go, Logan. Gabe had nothing to do with it."

I sigh in disgust. If Slate won't help, I'll just have to take care of it on my own, the way I planned.

It's the first time in my life that I've had trouble

going over plans for racing.

"So, is that it?" I ask when Slate sets down his paperwork.

"Yeah, for now."

I almost run out of the office, making a beeline for Gabe. He's elbow deep in 22's engine compartment.

"So, where were you last night?"

He straightens up in response to my question. "Fishing."

His terse answer fuels my anger. "Anybody with you?"

He scowls at me, clenching his grease-coated hands. "No, I always fish alone."

I nod, wishing someone would listen to me. But that's alright; I'll prove his guilt. Tonight.

– 10 –

"Hey, Mom! I'm going to ride my bike!" I shout up the stairs as eight o'clock draws near.

"Now? It's so hot!" she replies, her voice filtering down the stairs.

"Yeah, I'm heading out toward that old airfield, okay?"

"You have your phone?"

"Of course." I glance at it; it's 7:16. I'll have to pedal hard. Smith's field is a good eight miles from my house.

I zip past Gabe's house, craning my neck. Nobody is outside.

My front tire drops off the edge of the pavement, and I almost lose it. I force the bike back onto the road, wondering what will happen tonight.

I'll have to play it by ear. Sweat rolls off my forehead as I speed forward. According to the Internet, the airfield had shut down ten years ago. The long, smooth pavement makes for a perfect race track. The crucial skill would be acceleration, the ability to clutch in perfect harmony with the engine.

My nerves peak, making sweat flow. The driveway swings into view. It's overgrown, and even on my bike I have to duck under wild grape vines that hang down. Past the twisting drive, I see a few cars.

It's tough to swallow my pride at arriving on a bicycle, but I've got to pin Gabe for stealing Sophia, and this is the only way.

I peer through the overgrowth. Five big guys are gathered around a souped-up Nissan. It has a huge spoiler and hood scoops. Even with my anxiety, I'd love to drive that car.

A sharp laugh echoes; they've spotted me.

"Our driver's on a bike?"

I can't tell if the big guy in the center is angry or not, but the kid from the school bathroom comes over, fist bumping me like we're old buddies.

He leans close, his harsh tone meant for me alone. "You'd better be able to deliver, or you'll pay."

It's a pure threat. His entire reputation is riding on my performance.

"Just put me in the car." I jut my chin at it, my eyes searching everywhere for Sophia or Gabe. My muscles feel like jelly. She's nowhere in sight, and neither is he.

"I don't know about this," the boss man says.

I have to push this forward somehow. I need more time to find Sophia. I gauge the asphalt road. It looks like a quarter mile. "Give me eight seconds to prove it."

"You reach Toby on the other end in eight seconds, and you're in."

I look down the long black pavement with heat waves shimmering up from it. The guy holding the flag looks tiny from so far away. "Sure thing."

The boss crosses his meaty arms, nodding at the Nissan, and I start to doubt what I'm doing there. What if this is a total rabbit trail that isn't connected to Gabe or Sophia?

As I open the Nissan's door, I clear my throat. "Where's Gabe?"

"You know Gabe?" The boss man seems surprised.

"Course I do." Anger burns away everything else.

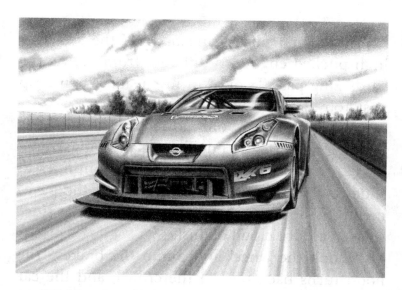

"He's at the shop tweaking up the *real* race car."

I nod, sliding into the small car. Its size conceals a racing machine.

A NOS button is on the dash, and an array of gauges makes me feel right at home. Even though I haven't driven a car with NOS before, I know it'll increase my engine's power for a moment. I'll have to time my boost just right. This will be an incredible eight seconds.

If it takes nine, my chances are fried. Pushing the start button, I grin, ready to shift. The boss holds up a hand, and when it falls, I clutch, shifting in rapid succession.

The Nissan pushes me back in the seat, the high-pitched engine so different from 77. As the yards zing past, I count in my head. When I rip past Toby, I'm on seven.

"Whoo!" I shout, only to realize the runway's running out fast, and I don't have any wings!

I lock up the brakes, but the car continues to slide toward the high grass. I sling off the pavement, still doing forty-five. The Nissan glides sideways in a thick cloud of dust.

I hook the wheel and pump the brakes. The hood turns back toward the crowd, and the car eases to a stop.

My chest heaving, I shift into first, inching out of the dirt. The elation of driving fades, and I brace for their anger at my losing control at the end.

The boss slams a heavy hand on the roof when I pull up. My heart almost stops, and I eye the passenger door as an escape hatch.

"Seven point four!" He yanks open the door, but my knees are too weak to stand as he towers over me. "Seven point four with the Nissan? Boys, we're taking this race home! Kid, be here tomorrow at eight o'clock sharp."

My stomach is in knots. This isn't the kind of

guy who's . . . *safe.*

"Gabe will be here then, right?" I say, my voice cracking.

He shrugs. "Yeah, of course, kid. He'll have the Ferrari ready for tomorrow."

I nod, doing my best to conceal my excitement. This will be worth it. I can return John's Ferrari and laptop, hopefully, tomorrow. Unfortunately, this means we'll be looking for a new mechanic again, but good riddance. Gabe hasn't earned this opportunity if he's the kind of person who steals. I hop onto my bike and pedal like mad for home, doing a measly 13 mph.

- 11 -

The day creeps past like ten laps with the caution flag. It's Saturday, and without school to take up the hours, my nerves ramp higher. I've checked my phone battery and storage somewhere around 900 times already. I just need a photo of Gabe with Sophia; then John will believe me when I return his car. But what will happen when Gabe sees me? It makes my stomach feel like I just ate gear lube.

I stretch my legs. I'd better be ready to run. Something tells me these guys aren't keen on anybody knowing what they're doing—stealing cars and holding races.

I click open my phone and flinch. It's 7:05!

"Mom!" I shout on my way out the door. "I'll be

back later. I'm gonna take a bike ride to the same place as yesterday."

It's strange, heading to a race without my gear. Sweat rolls down my face as I funnel all of my nervous energy into my bike's pedals.

I sure wish I'd brought some water; my tongue is stuck to the roof of my mouth when I glimpse the airstrip tucked away in the woods.

"This one's for you, John," I whisper, turning into the drive. Two muscular guys step out at the first turn, and I almost flip the bike at their sudden appearance.

"Buzz off, kid," one says, flexing his massive arms.

"But—"

"I said, get!"

"But I'm the driver!" I protest.

"Yeah, and I'm the president of the US of A."

I wish I'd gotten the boss's name. Something deep inside tells me I should just head home, but I jam it down.

"I'd hate to see what you got coming when I tell them you wouldn't let me in." It takes every drop of determination to stare him down.

"Slim, go get KT."

The other guy strides off around the bend. I try not to hyperventilate in the eternity it takes for the kid from the school bathroom to show up. My shoulders loosen as he appears.

"Bro, you're late!" he yells.

"That's not my fault." I cock my head toward the muscular guy, who now looks uneasy.

"Come on," KT says. "The first race is in five."

I nod, double checking that I have my phone. We pass the last of the thick vegetation, and I stifle a grunt. Sophia is right there, pristine. A plain white trailer sits behind her. I pull up my phone, acting as if I'm sending a text. The picture I take even catches the license plate on the trailer. A crowd who looks like they belong at a tattoo festival surround the runway. But Sophia is here, and that must mean Gabe is nearby.

I look around. Souped-up cars line the pavement, including the Nissan from yesterday. A shadow looms over my shoulder.

"Hey, kid, here's the deal . . . " The boss is even more intimidating in a T-shirt with the sleeves cut off, a thick silver chain around his neck. "We're running elimination matches. The fastest car races again. Top prize is the car that comes in second place plus ten grand. I'll give you a cut when you win it for me. Seven point four seconds! Let's see you do that again."

"Hey . . ." I force the word past my dry throat. "Where's Gabe?"

"No time for chitchat. You're late. Just get in."

He shoves me toward Sophia. I slide in, and my eyebrows go up. Sophia's gotten some upgrades. A NOS button and a set of extra gauges ringed in soft blue lights are on the dash. There won't be time on this short track to use the NOS, but I run my finger over it with reverence.

"Okay," I say to Sophia. She's already running, and the boss is on the pavement, motioning me forward next to another racer. "We'll just run once till I get that shot of Gabe. Then I'm out of here."

Talking to Sophia makes me feel better. I flick the paddle shifter on the steering wheel into first, lining Sophia's bumper up on the starting line. A shiver runs down my spine at her intense power.

A smile breaks through the nerves, tipping up one side of my mouth. Sitting in Sophia is amazing, but now I'm going to race her!

I line up with a yellow twin-turbo Toyota Supra. On the left, a lady holds a green flag.

I settle my fingers on the wheel. The long, straight strip of runway calls me forward. When the flag drops, everything else fades. I shift through the gears at light-speed. Sophia can do zero to sixty in two point five seconds, but I shave off another tenth.

Her engine's perfect balance has no bounds, and seconds later, I flash past the waving checkered flag at the end. I gasp, pulling up from the deep focus, expecting a turn, but this is no racetrack! The brakes lock up, and I slide over the grass, hooking around like I did yesterday as she slides to a stop.

A cloud of dust envelops the car. "That was amazing!" I shout.

The dust blows aside, and far down the track I see the boss leaping high with one fist pumping in the air.

"Sophia, something tells me we did good," I say, rubbing her dash as I ease out of the dirt and back to the starting line before rolling down my window.

"Six point one!" the boss says as he leans on the window frame. "Kid, where you been all my life? You can drive!"

A crew steps forward, using soft rags to wipe the dust from Sophia. Something tells me they've done this before. A hot-pink Mitsubishi Eclipse pulls up. The exhaust rips the air, but I can hear the whine of turbos as the female driver pumps the gas. The girl scowls at me, running one finger across her neck.

I can't stay here. This is crazy.

"Where's Gabe?" I ask the boss.

"He just pulled up. But you got another run. Don't let this chick freak you out, man. You've got this."

I open my mouth to protest, but he's already in front of Sophia, lining us up again. Just one more run, then I'll catch Gabe and get out of there. A glance over at the pink car proves to be a mistake. The girl's snarling at me like an escaped zoo animal.

The next thing I know, the flag drops, and I'm popping through gears, the motion as familiar as breathing. The pink car holds by my fender, not giving an inch!

Then Sophia hits the power band, and we surge ahead at the last second.

I brake earlier this time but still end up in the dirt. The pink car spins farther away, as if it's on ice. I make a quick escape from her and return to the starting line for safety.

A neon-blue Honda Civic is waiting there, revving his engine. It looks like they dumped $5,000 of upgrades into a $200 car. Somehow it still sounds threatening.

The dusters are back, fawning over Sophia as if she's royalty.

The boss taps my window and leans in. "Bro, nice run. Hey, did I mention what happens if you lose? You got two more races, and if you end up second on the last one and lose me this car, it's gonna be bad for you, man."

"No," I reply, swallowing hard, "you didn't mention that."

He flexes, his forearms bulging near my head. "Well, now you know. Before you ask, there's Gabe."

He nods to one side, and I scan the crowd, reaching for my phone. "Where?"

I don't see Gabe anywhere among them.

"Bro, he's got the same spikes as always."

A tall Caucasian man with bleached blonde hair that stands up in six huge spikes is the only person he could mean.

"Him?" I ask, the blood draining from my face as I realize my mistake. *Have I let my hatred for Gabe convince me of a fairy tale?* I still don't have any actual evidence that he was involved in the theft.

"Get your head in the game, kid. You've got to win, remember?"

A high-pitched laugh escapes me as the boss smacks Sophia's hood, making me blink. "Sophia?" I whisper as I roll up the window and grip the wheel. "We need to leave. Now!"

My eyes run across the rough crowd, the boss's threat pulsing in my brain. A thousand thoughts collide, jumbling together.

What made me think I had this figured out? Why didn't I call the police as soon as I saw Sophia? I grit my teeth in realization. I didn't do it because I wanted to pin Gabe so badly that I couldn't see straight. But he's not here. And I was wrong.

I cringe. My mom thinks I'm still on my bike.

Sweat makes the shifter slick under my hand. The Civic surges forward. I didn't even see the flag drop!

I floor it, gaining on the Civic as if the boss were on my heels.

"What do I do?" I scream over the engine as I hit sixth gear and blow past the Civic. I hit the dirt at full speed, fishtailing in a wild arc.

When the dust clears, a figure leaps from the woods. It's Gabe, and his phone is pointed right at me!

– 12 –

As Gabe snaps a series of photos his expression is dark. Shocked, I roll down the window.

"Ha! I knew you were involved in this somehow!" Gabe shouts. "What's wrong with you, rich boy? John hasn't done enough for you, so you gotta steal his car to race even more?"

"What?" I cry as I lean out the window, but the rest of my words jam in my throat.

"A rich kid like you must think you can get away with anything. You're gonna pay now, Logan!"

Pay. That word makes me flinch. I look down the runway, my mouth hanging open. I can't go back there, knowing Gabe didn't steal Sophia. This is what my parents meant when they told me not to get involved with the wrong crowd. Well, here I sit, smack dab in the epicenter of a wrong crowd volcano.

I rev Sophia's smooth-as- glass engine, my hands sweating as I search for a solution.

Gabe's here to prove that *I* stole Sophia. It's obvious he didn't do it.

"Hey!" The guy holding the checkered flag looks from me to Gabe with a scowl. Five or six other guys step forward, way too close for comfort.

"Oh, man," I say, my foot still pumping the gas.

"Why's he filming us?" one of them shouts, pointing at Gabe. "Does anybody know that kid?"

Gabe's face grows pale as he stuffs the phone in his pocket.

Five of them sprint toward us. My heart slams into my toes. Gabe stands frozen, a growing look of horror on his face.

"Get in the car, Gabe!" I shout, shifting into first. Sophia spits a plume of dirt, tires spinning as I slide up to Gabe.

He flinches as if he forgot I was there.

"Hurry!" I scream as the guys close in on us.

He rips open the door and slides in. I shift into second, Sophia's massive torque creating a spec-

tacular fishtail. I crank the wheel into each slide, switching directions until I'm back in control.

Gabe braces himself against the dash. "You didn't steal this car?"

"No! I came here to prove you did!"

We scowl at each other. One goon smacks the rear fender as we surge past. The truth settles inside Sophia's plush cab: we're in *deep* trouble.

"Drive!" he shouts.

I point the hood at the narrow four-wheeler path, our only escape. Branches slap Sophia's perfect paint.

"Sorry, John!" I cringe as roots clang against the

undercarriage. I push the front-end lift button, but the extra inch and a half of clearance can't cope with the rough trail.

"Well, if you didn't steal her and I didn't steal her, then who did?" Gabe asks, one hand gripping the handhold as he stares in the rearview.

"Those guys!" I shout.

We hit a sandy pothole. Bam! The hood ricochets skyward. Gabe and I scream like tea kettles, branches slapping, engine roaring.

As we slam back down to earth, I struggle to keep Sophia on the narrow trail.

My eyes flick to the rearview mirror, and my heart skips a beat.

Bits of bright paint flash through the trees behind us.

"Ah!"

"What?" Gabe shouts, scanning the path ahead.

"We got company!" I roar.

He twists around, hands white knuckled on the headrest. "This is bad."

He straightens out as we ramp off another root, then grunts as we bottom out. The damage to Sophia is growing with each heartbeat.

I glance at the blue-lit gauge cluster. She's still running fine, which means we have a chance. Ahead, the trail splits. I clench my jaw. Doing 35 mph through the woods doesn't leave me time for clear thinking. The pink car surges up to our rear bumper.

"Left! Take the left!" Gabe shouts, pointing.

"Okay!" I crank the wheel at the last second. The pink car turns hard, but its bumper catches a pine tree, and it spins sideways across the trail, blocking the others.

"Whoo-hoo!" we shout together. Then the past comes rushing back as we scowl at each other.

The trail is even narrower, with sharp, blind turns.

"Look for John's laptop!" I yell, as we careen into a puddle. Muck sprays through my open window. I hunch forward, trying to find the wiper switch.

"It's that button!" Gabe points to the dash, which is covered in knobs and switches. Sophia's right fender scrapes against a tree trunk. Gabe cringes, pulling away from the impact. He reaches over and flicks the wipers on.

They clear the windshield just in time to reveal the yellow Supra roaring straight toward Gabe's door from another trail!

"Go!" he yells, covering his head.

I floor it, and Sophia pushes us back in our seats

as we zoom past, sticks and dirt flying. We're just ahead of the Supra as it swerves on the trail behind.

"John's laptop, we have to find it!" I yell, tendons straining in my neck as I notch up our speed.

Gabe grunts, contorting to reach underneath his seat. "It's not here!"

"Check my side." It's the most important thing to John, especially now that I'm destroying Sophia more and more with each passing second.

A glance in the rearview reveals two more racers swerving onto the trail. "This isn't good!"

Tall pine trees sweep past. It feels more like a video game than real life—except for the all-too-real smack of branches hitting the car.

Gabe is tossed around as he reaches over the middle console. He pats under my seat, his face mashed against my knee.

We hit another pothole. Gabe's ribs slam into the dash, and his head smacks against the wheel.

"Ah!" I shout. I knee him hard, freeing the steering wheel just in time to avoid a gigantic oak. As Gabe falls back, the engine screams, but the car slows.

"Oh, no!"

– 13 –

Frantic, I search the gauges for the reason Sophia's going nowhere. *Maybe we scraped off the transmission lines!* The yellow car slams into us, driving us sideways.

Years of habit make me flick the shifter. It's in neutral! Gabe must've knocked it out of gear when he was looking for the laptop. I flick it into third and roar away from the car that's shoving us from behind.

Gabe grimaces as he points left again, and we dive into another tight turn, spitting twin plumes of dirt. That's when I remember something Slate told me.

"John has a secret compartment!" I shout.

"Check the seat for anything that looks like a button!"

I hear a click and then Gabe lofts a black laptop case into the air. "Got it!"

"Yes!" I yell, slapping the steering wheel. "Now we're talking."

Hope surges, knowing there's a chance to return it to John—if we make it out of there.

Then my lightning-fast brain kicks into gear. "Call Slate. Call *somebody!*"

Gabe fumbles for his phone. "Slate! Logan and I are in trouble! We're being chased near the old airfield!"

The yellow car surges forward, slamming us again. We both shout as I struggle with the wheel. The trees are nothing but a blur as I fly down the path.

"We're in Sophia! We need help!" Gabe shouts into the phone.

Driving off road at these speeds, I can't let anything distract me. I condense, letting every fiber of my being focus on the trail, the engine, the speed.

We ramp over a raised grass-covered road. The hood tilts skyward, and all four wheels are off the ground! I grip the steering wheel, knowing it's going to be a rough landing.

Sophia bottoms out, her rear tires catching on

the edge of the road. We dive over the far side. The damp grass on the steep ledge is like ice.

I wrestle Sophia as she almost flips, but she leaps back onto the wide road.

"Yes!" I cry. The wide-open grass road stretches ahead like a beacon of hope. Our lead increases now that we have a good stretch with no trees around. After another few minutes of driving, a fence appears on the horizon. It's the end of the airport!

"There's Slate!" Gabe yells, pointing past the tall fence ahead.

Slate's white pickup flashes past on the state road beyond the fence, then disappears beyond the trees between us. He must live nearby to be there so soon, but boy, am I glad to see him!

"There's an exit! It's how I got in!" Gabe shouts, clutching the case as he points toward another narrow trail. The racers fall farther back on the straightaway; they can't compete with Sophia's power.

I downshift, turning hard, and we dive toward the trail. Leaves slap, leaving no time to think. Reflex takes over as we flash past a broken gate, then skid on the main road.

Slate's white truck barrels straight toward us!

"Aah!" I crank the wheel. Slate's truck slides

to the side of the road. Sophia squeals to a stop, facing Slate.

Gabe and I sit, our chests pumping as we stare over the dented hood. Gabe nods once. "Nice driving, man."

Slate leaps from his truck and rushes toward us on the quiet road. "Logan! Gabe! What on earth is going on?"

I can't tell if he's angry or *really* angry. The roar of engines echoes on the trail to our right. Slate's hand is on Sophia's roof as four bright colored racers careen onto the road, surrounding us.

"Boys," Slate whispers, "what's going on here?"

Two drivers get out, their muscles bunching up as they slam their fists into their palms.

"Um . . . ," I say, my eyes locked on the closest one. "That would take way too long to explain."

Slate spreads his hands, turning toward the men. "Easy now, boys. Let's talk this out."

"We ain't here to talk."

"Logan, move over," Slate whispers.

"What?" Sophia is a two-seater, and both seats are full.

"Now," Slate growls. One goon is a few steps away.

"One." Slate's voice is so low I almost miss it.

"Two."

I coil up, ready to launch over the console.

"Three!"

I explode in the small space, my legs tangling with the steering wheel as Sophia's door whips open behind me, and I land in Gabe's lap.

"Ow!"

"Oomph!" My face smashes against the cold mud-stained window. Then Sophia rockets forward, and I crush the air out of Gabe's lungs.

Since my cheek is sharing molecules with the glass, I get a super-clear view of the yellow Supra's fender, which flashes past with less than an inch of clearance.

Slate runs Sophia through her gears. The front wheels have a wobble that didn't exist before, but Slate drives like a Formula 1 racer. I twist, searching for balance, kneeing Gabe in the stomach.

"Come on, man!" he groans.

"Sorry!" I reply, cringing.

I end up sitting on his lap, my head smashed against the roof, knees against my chest, the laptop case poking me in the pancreas.

Slate glares at the rearview mirror. "Not today, boys."

Gabe and I glance at each other, then peer out the rear window. A familiar string of cars is right behind us.

Slate pushes the NOS button, Sophia leaps forward, the wobble making every fiber shimmy.

A Honda van sweeps around the bend ahead, coming toward us. I squint, feeling like a pretzel. "Is that . . . " My heart sinks as the van grows closer, the driver and passenger becoming clear.

"Piper?" Gabe squeaks, his voice a perfect reflection of my own horror.

Her pretty mouth opens, and she leans forward inside the van, her head cocked to one side as we zip past. I groan, twisting to ensure the van gets through the pursuing group.

"Why did it have to be her?" Gabe moans.

The NOS runs out, but it gained us enough distance from the pack to enter town at a safe speed. As we turn onto busier roads, the other drivers ride our bumper, trying to force us into a spinout.

Sophia jerks, taking a hard hit, but Slate proves his skill by holding her solid.

"We're home, boys!" Slate shouts as he downshifts, hooking the wheel. Sophia's front wheels lock up while the rear wheels squeal, sliding into a parallel parking space in front of the police station.

I get a glimpse of the Civic's driver making a fist, his teeth bared as he zips past. Blue and red lights flash as three police cars peel out after the racers.

We sit there, just breathing as officers surround Sophia.

"Mr. Emery, are you alright?" Officer Wells asks as he leans in the window. "This wouldn't be John Taylor's stolen car, would it?" He frowns as he takes in the damage. Pine boughs are sticking out of her hood, and her crinkled hood is caked with blobs of mud.

Slate looks over at us, smashed into the tiny space.

"Boys, you've got some explaining to do."

– 14 –

I sit in my room, staring at my phone. When it rings, that sound might signal the end of my racing career.

I swallow the boulder of worry that's lodged in my throat. Blinded by my desire to prove Gabe was a thief, I had ignored the fact that the airstrip race was unsanctioned and could jeopardize my racing license. *What was I thinking?*

Breathing is an effort as I sit in silence. What if they yank my license? The bleak view of that future crushes me inside. How could I have been so stupid?

My phone rings. Finally.

I stare at the screen, which displays Slate's name, but I'm frozen in place. It rings and rings, then goes quiet.

"What's wrong with you?" I growl at myself, snatching my phone and calling him back. I squeak out just one word. "Hey."

"Okay, Logan, I just got off the phone with SCCA." I wince—that's who issued my racing license.

Slate sighs, then rustles some papers. "Here's the deal: if you had driven in a race on a public road, you'd be toast. It's a good thing we met on the road when we did. Anyway, since you only drove on private property, there won't be any charges, and your license isn't affected. Turns out the property is owned by Hank Rankin's uncle, so they had permission to be there. It's just not zoned for racing."

A high-pitched sigh escapes, and I fall back on my bed, the phone still pressed to my ear.

"Let's never do that again." Slate's dry tone makes me laugh.

"Sir, yes, sir!" Relief floods through my veins.

"Hey," Slate adds, "with that behind us, John is thrilled to have that laptop back. It's possible that what you did was worth it. No, forget I said that."

I nod, as if he can see it. "That's good. I'll be sure to forget it. What about Sophia?"

"The insurance company totaled her."

I cringe, hating that I'm responsible for it.

"But John will buy her back from the insurance company. He plans to keep her as a showpiece just the way she is as a memorial to his team's extreme efforts to get her back."

A laugh clears the last of the sour feeling inside. "See you tomorrow, Slate."

- 15 -

It's 5:05 pm. Slate's arms are crossed as he stares out the shop door. I check my phone. Gabe is six minutes late. Not great for his second week on the job.

Soon, Slate starts pacing, and I resort to organizing the toolbox. I was hoping Gabe and I would get a fresh start, but maybe he's decided that he's

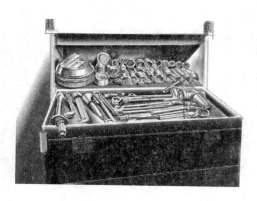

done with Taylor Racing.

Slate runs a hand through his hair. "That's it. I'm calling him."

I glance at my phone. It's 5:15. Slate doesn't tolerate lateness.

I straighten when Slate pulls his phone away from his ear. All the way across the shop, I hear a string of wild Spanish echoing through it.

"Whoa! Slow down, Gabe." Slate eases the phone back to his ear. I edge closer, my pulse spiking.

"She's missing?" He listens and then nods. "For how long?" Then Slate shoves his phone into his pocket.

"Logan, get in the truck. Gabe's little sister is lost."

A hundred questions race through my mind as I climb into Slate's big diesel.

"She's two and a half years old, been gone for hours," he says, cranking the engine.

"What have the police done so far?"

"Nothing. His mom's terrified of them. She probably has some immigration paperwork that's not quite complete. So they haven't called it in." We peel out of the shop drive. Tall pines flash past as his engine roars.

"What do we do?" I ask, my stomach feeling

like a grease pit.

"Find her." Slate's order fills my mind. I nod, unable to fathom having a little sister, much less what it would feel like to know she's lost. We clip past my house, *possibly* going over the speed limit. Slate breaks hard, and we whip into Gabe's driveway.

The scattered trailers, bare dirt, and cars are all empty. Everyone's gathered by one trailer with random-sized pieces of plywood covering its base.

I stare at Gabe. Will he scream at me to leave? We didn't have a chance to sort things out after the incident with Sophia. Everything inside me is off balance, and I have no idea what to expect. Slate gets out, approaching the small group of people. Gabe rakes one hand across his red eyes, worry etched on his face.

I open the door, bracing myself. Gabe and his family bear a striking resemblance to one another, and they're all talking in Spanish.

Slate holds up his hands, quieting them. "Where does she like to play?"

"Mary play at river!" a tiny woman says through her tears. Gabe wraps one arm around her shoulders, and I'm certain she's his mother.

Slate's face goes pale as he looks toward the White

Oak River. "Okay, where have you already searched?"

Gabe repeats the words in Spanish, and people point and talk all at once. I ease up to the group. Its obvious chaos has reigned over the search.

"Take it easy!" Slate strides over to an SUV with a thick coating of dust on its rear window.

With one finger, he draws a crude map of the area. "You three, search here!"

Two boys about my age and an older girl study the section Slate draws. "Si!"

I admire Slate's ability to make things simple. He continues until it's just Gabe, Slate, and me standing there.

"This is our section." He outlines a rectangle covering the north edge of the river. "Gabe?"

He's a mess. I can see his hands trembling from here. "Yeah?"

"If we don't find her in an hour, I'm calling the sheriff."

He nods. "Si, sounds good."

"Okay, spread out, and be sure we cover every square inch of our territory."

I give the sky a long look. North Carolina is almost always sunny, but deep, dark clouds hang over the Atlantic Ocean a scant mile away.

"She's afraid of storms!" Gabe says, watching the sky. "We have to find her!" As we set off for the river's edge, I grimace. A girl that small and that much water sweeping toward the ocean? It's a terrible combination. I see why Gabe is shaking.

We spread out as we approach the reeds. They've always bothered me; seems like gators must be lurking there. I wish I'd asked someone if gators live in North Carolina. I shake the tension from my shoulders, gritting my teeth.

Remembering when I got lost in the mall as a child, I scan the darkening clouds. I still dream of it sometimes. *We've got to find her.*

Then a thought strikes me. "Gabe! What is she wearing?"

I brace for his usual hatred.

"A white shirt and purple shorts!" Desperation fills his voice as it echoes from the undergrowth.

"Okay," I whisper, "I can do this." I step into the marsh, my shoes squishing in thick mud. Ahead, something rustles. "Mary?"

There's no response. Then a huge bird takes off, its brilliant white wings beating the air. Its strange screeching cry makes goosebumps rise along my arms. I duck as a flash of lightning highlights the rolling black clouds.

"Perfect." I shake my head, pushing forward. The storm is making *me* nervous. What about a two-year-old girl? I veer toward the river's edge, seeking an easier way through the sharp-edged reeds.

A kid would take the path of least resistance. I'm surprised to find the water is far away, a wide span of mud stretching from the reeds to the river.

Some of the mud is cracked, but closer to the water it's slick and shiny. Something ahead catches my attention. I trudge forward, clinging to the plants where the roots provide a better place to walk. Then I realize what the object is—a tiny shoe!

Rushing forward, I pull it from the muck.

"Mary?" I shout, listening hard. "Slate, I found her shoe!" My heart slams as I call at the top of my lungs. But the storm's towering over me now, its swirling wind tossing my hair and snatching the words away.

I hold her shoe, caught in indecision. I dare not leave her trail, not now with a thunderstorm rolling closer, bolts of lightning flashing everywhere.

"Gabe!" I listen hard, but the wind swallows every other sound.

I press ahead, the muck clinging to my boots.

Flashes of lightning make me flinch, and the air feels charged with a wild energy.

The swirling wind brings a snatch of a screeching cry to my ears. I freeze. Was that the bird?

"Mary!" I yell, my chest heaving.

The cry comes again, and I race forward, barely able to keep my balance on the slimy mud. The increasing darkness makes me long for a flashlight. Then a dot of white shows up in a flash of lightning.

"Mary!" It sure looks like the bird I spooked earlier. I stare across the distance. There's nothing but slimy, cracked muck. A kid couldn't go that far. The white speck is near the waterline. I turn, moving farther down the riverbank.

The cry comes again, making my hair stand on end. That's no bird! When I turn back, the small dot is outlined against the looming storm. It's her!

I shout for Slate and Gabe, but the blasting wind overcomes my voice, drawing it out over the river. She's at the water's edge, and time is running out! I plunge into the mud, slogging toward Mary. Soon, I'm covered from head to toe, slipping again and again on the stinking riverbed. Sharp drops of rain smack into my skin.

"Not now!" I shout at the sky.

Mary's cries are weak; that's why she'd sounded like a bird. Things look worse the closer I get. She's buried to her waist, which makes her look so small. Plus, she seems disoriented, her movements jerky.

"Mary, it's okay. I'm here to help you!" I yell into the wind as I draw closer. But I'm not so sure. My legs sink deeper with every step toward the white-capped river.

At least the rain quits. *For now.* Downriver, I can't see past the wall of water falling from the sky. *You'd better hurry, Logan.*

My muscles burning, I pull my right leg out of the muck, which slurps as it loses its grip. Terror makes me freeze as my left leg sinks deeper than before. When will it stop? I'm a few feet away, close enough to see Mary's terror.

"I'm coming!" I shout. The distance from the safety of the reeds seems like miles. I stretch forward, my muck-covered hand clasping hers.

"Got you!" I whisper, grimacing as lightning crackles in the air. She's crying, clawing at me in terror.

Gripping her proves challenging. The mud has her in its clutches, and her skin is slick. It's like trying to hold on to a fish.

I've sunk to my waist, and my heart is pounding as the storm rages closer and closer. I dig one hand deep into the mud, my fingers reaching her knee, and I work it free.

"Okay!" My voice is trembling. I wish I could be strong for her. Struggling to free her has forced both of my legs deeper. Fear races up my spine. I jam it down and dig again. With a groan, I pull. She cries out in pain, but her leg comes free!

"You're out!" The wind sucks the words from my lips like a vacuum cleaner.

Mary clings to me, which reveals how bad our position is. She's as tall as me now, her weight pressing me deeper yet. Plus, she's sinking again too!

My legs are numb from the cold mud's icy grip. The wind goes still for a heartbeat.

I'm stuck.

Completely stuck.

I twist. The shore is so far behind us, and it's almost dark under the boiling clouds just above. I'm hyperventilating as everything spins.

"Mama!" Mary buries her face in my neck, longing for safety.

"Mary, run for shore!"

She shakes her head, crying. Then she focuses

on something behind me, and her muddy finger points toward shore. "Gabe!"

At her cry, I almost collapse. Twisting around, I can just make out his outline near shore. "He's coming!"

He proves far wiser than me, however, choosing a longer trail and sticking to the harder, cracked mud. Soon, he's only a few yards away, but the soft, slimy muck might be an impenetrable barrier between us.

"Mary!" he cries, holding out his arms. The shiny mud reflects the lightning bolts above. I peel Mary's thin arms from my neck, shoving her toward him. "Go!"

She teeters, pulling back as even her light weight forces her into the mud. I lift her high and scoot her forward, biting my lip to keep from crying out as I sink even deeper.

A crack of thunder rattles my chest. It seems to give Mary wings. Her legs churn, and she falls, crawling toward Gabe. He snatches her arm. "Come on, Logan!"

"Can't!" I'm on the verge of puking, realizing how bad the situation is. "I'm stuck!"

He stares at me for a second, his teeth bared as

he clutches his little sister. Then he takes off running like a deer for shore, sinking ankle deep in the muck.

"Gabe!" I scream, but it's useless. He can't hear me. Time slows down as I watch them race away, slipping in the deeper spots of mud. He's made his choice . . . to save his sister. A frosty hand of fear closes around my heart. I twist back toward the wind-tossed river. It's better than watching him disappear.

I can't blame him; I've never had a sibling. The bond between them is special. I look skyward, feeling the mud inching up toward my belly button.

With a grimace, I fight off tears. The sky lets loose, making them invisible. Rain fills the cracks in the mud and rises around my ribs.

"No . . . No!" Nothing I do can change the water's slow advance. I'm alone. Truly alone.

I clench my fists and yell at the storm. The sound grows into a bellow that rises to a war cry.

I feel better for a second until the storm answers back, tearing the air apart. A snatch of a voice on the wind makes me turn.

Gabe and Slate are racing along the reeds! Both of them are carrying something large above their heads, but I can't make it out in the pounding rain.

I scream like mad as Gabe splashes into the mud. The rain has covered it now, making it all a slick pool of slime.

He came back.

Something breaks loose inside as I watch him sprint toward me. I've never been so excited to see a person in my life. Then I realize what they're carrying—plywood!

The wind snatches at it like a giant sail, and they struggle for balance. Slate's longer legs out-pace Gabe, carrying him nearer.

"Wait!" Gabe shouts as Slate draws near. "Don't go any closer!"

Already, Slate's bulk forces him knee deep. Gabe slams his piece of wood onto the mud, and Slate hops onto it, then lays his piece down. Their bridge reaches within an inch of my chest.

I claw at it, but I can't budge my legs. Slate's wide hands grip my armpits and he roars, pulling hard.

I grimace in pain. It feels like he's tearing me in half!

"Stop! You'll never get him out like that!" Gabe screams over the storm. He pulls a strange-looking power tool from its strap over his shoulder. It's got a long hose with a blunt end.

"What's that?" Slate shouts. I can barely hear him even though he's inches away.

"Concrete vibrator! Hurry!" Gabe skids on his muddy knees to the edge of the wood, jamming the tube down my right side. He forces it lower, and I feel the metal tip inching toward my knee. He turns the tool on, and the muck vibrates.

"Slate, pull this leg, slowly. Give the mud time to loosen!"

Together, Slate and Gabe dig at my right leg, pulling it up. It's agonizingly slow.

"Hurry!" Slate's panicked voice urges.

I look up, blinking away the rain. The storm's fury has passed, leaving behind a cold, heavy blanket of air. One leg is almost out. We're not in danger of being fried by lightning anymore. Things seem better, not worse. My thoughts become muddled as I watch Slate and Gabe. They share a sharp glance, then dive for my left leg.

I'm still puzzled by their panic. Then I look at the water and stifle a shout.

– 16 –

The White Oak River is at my chest. It's not just rainfall; the river is rising!

Huge, heaving breaths grip me. The tide! I'm tilted hard to one side, my right leg free, but the muck won't let go of my left leg no matter how hard I struggle.

Gabe shakes his head. "Stay still, Logan. The tide is rising; every time you move, you sink deeper. You've got to trust us!"

A wave smacks my shoulder. If I don't stay still, I might be trapped forever. Taking a deep breath, I force myself to go limp as their frantic tugging twists my leg. I glance toward the shore. The high-water line is above my current position. When the tide is in, I'll be four feet under.

"Hurry!"

With a roar, Slate grips my knee and pulls. I don't care how bad it hurts!

With a loud slurp, my shoeless foot comes free. I splash onto the plywood next to Gabe and Slate, pain pulsing in my legs. But the river's still creeping higher, and the muck between us and shore looks like an impassable distance.

Slate's meaty hands pull me to my feet, and I can't contain a shout as pins and needles sting like a million bees. I wince; there's no sensation at all in my legs other than that!

"I can't tell where my feet are!" I shout, confirming their presence by looking down. The water's almost knee deep!

"There's no time!" Slate hollers, taking my arm and slinging it over his shoulder. "Gabe, move forward. You get the piece of wood behind and move ahead. We'll have to leapfrog out of here!"

Slate drags me forward; my legs are useless.

The board tilts under our weight, sinking deeper.

"Hurry!" Slate bellows in my ear.

Gabe is on his knees, his hands deep in the water and muck. "I . . . Ah! I can't budge it!"

"Switch with me!"

Gabe stands up. We're all dripping mud. He grabs my other wrist and pulls my arm over his shoulder. I recoil, trying to stand on my own, but the flaring pain from the pins and needles won't let me.

Gabe adjusts his slimy grip. "I've got you, Logan."

The words make me freeze. Covered in sludge, the water rising by the second, he's right there with me, risking everything. Maybe we *can* overcome the past.

"I thought you left for good."

He nods. "I knew I couldn't get you out without the cement vibrator. I took a Coast Guard class on quicksand last year."

Quicksand. The word makes me shiver.

Slate's roar morphs into a grunt. "Come on!" he shouts at the plywood.

One corner tips up from the water. The mud is like glue as Slate's muscles bunch up, and the wood pulls free. He throws the board toward shore. It lands with a wet smack, and we shuffle onto it.

The plywood shoots forward like a surfboard, and Gabe struggles to balance us both.

Slate is back on his knees, pulling up the last board.

"We can't stay ahead of the water at this rate!" I shout.

"Look!" Gabe juts his chin toward shore as he uses both hands to hold me up.

A long string of men and boys are sprinting along the river's edge! They're all carrying plywood sections over their heads.

"They found us!" The relief in Gabe's voice breaks fear's grip on my heart.

Slate gives up on the sunken plywood, and we stand with the White Oak River rising around our thighs, watching Gabe's family. In quick succession, they slap their sections over the mud. A wooden trail grows by the second, sinking under the water.

"Rapido!" a man cries, motioning us forward.

Gabe doesn't waste a second, dragging me behind him. The boards slip and slide, so Slate takes my other arm, and soon we're right there at the reeds that had always terrified me. Now they seem like home, the safest place on earth!

Everyone's talking at once, a jumbled mixture of English and Spanish. By the time we reach the yard, the pins and needles are fading, replaced by an intense burning sensation. On a sparse patch of wet grass, Gabe, Slate, and I flop down, staring at the blue sky. We lie there, just breathing, so thankful for solid ground.

"Well," I say, panting. "That was terrifying."

By then the women have rushed out of the house, and they're all patting my face, shoulders, and arms. I struggle into a sitting position, groaning as I grip my legs.

Gabe's mom crouches in front of me, speaking in Spanish.

"She says she's grateful to you . . . more than words can say . . . " Gabe translates, trying to keep up with her words. "Mary is safe because of you . . . Anything you need, if you ever need help . . . the Silva family will be there for you."

Tears course down her face, and she pulls me into a tight hug. Over her shoulder, I notice the mobile home no longer has anything around its base.

"Um, did you rip your house apart to save me?"

Gabe looks over his shoulder at it. "No worries. We'll find something else to cover it with."

It's strange to sit there talking to him.

Soon, the women have a line of pots full of warm water for us to wash with.

"We can just use the hose," Slate says.

But they won't hear of it. I stand, but my feet feel like over-filled balloons. I wobble. After Slate and I are rinsed, I have to sit down. Like *now*.

I make it to his truck, then hesitate because I'm still dripping.

"Just get in." The truck rocks as Slate gets in, soaking his seat.

As he puts the truck in gear, I lean my head back. The reality of what happened settles in, and I bite back hot tears.

Slate pulls out, but I know I'm different from when we arrived. It's only a mile to my house where I'll be safe and warm.

"Logan, you did good." Slate's deep voice breaks loose a flood of emotions.

"That's the scariest thing that's ever happened to me." I keep my eyes closed, trying to control my thoughts.

"Fear is a funny thing," Slate says. "It can kill you . . . or save you."

"How's that?"

"Well, fear keeps you from jumping off a ten-story building, which keeps you safe. But fear can also cripple you and keep you from doing hard things. Things like you did today. Fear can seep in, especially at the track. Start squashing today's replays in your head as soon as they begin."

"Replays?" My body's empty, sagging into the seat.

"Your brain wants to replay something like this. People get stuck looking back, and that gives fear free rein. It spreads like a poison to other parts of your life. It won't stay contained in the mud and water you experienced today. You have to choose what you think about, so you're controlling your life instead of fear."

He pulls right up to my door. "I'd better explain what happened," he says, hopping out.

I look down at my soaked clothes, wondering if my legs can hold me up long enough to reach our front door.

- 17 -

The next day passes in a rush. Mom keeps me home from school, insisting I see a doctor. He tells us what I already knew: my legs will be sore for a few days. *Thanks a lot.*

At home I hunt for a quiet place to think. I lie on the garage floor. My legs feel like rubber bands that have been stretched too far. The cool concrete looks inviting against the hot pain in my body.

Easing down, I lie spread-eagled and sigh. The immense room holds a single toolbox against the wall. Dreams fill my head. I'm driving 77, pulling ahead of the pack. Time is irrelevant as the cold from the concrete soaks into my skin.

The door opens, but I don't look up. Mom's

been hovering all day. When she doesn't come in, I twist around, only to discover it's Gabe and Slate standing there! My face feels hot as I ease up. "Ow."

Being still made the pain worse. Gabe looks down, embarrassed, but Slate strides in like nothing's wrong. "Gabe said you weren't in school. You alright?"

"Sure, just sore. Mom was worried."

He nods, looking around the garage. "This place could use some cars."

"Exactly what I've been thinking."

"So, I talked to John." Slate rubs his jaw.

My heartbeat picks up in response to his tone. "And?"

"He wants to enter the Star's National Series."

"The . . . that's a super late model series," I stutter, stating the obvious and sounding foolish. But it's an enormous opportunity! Plus, it's a series, which means we'd be gaining points with every race, working toward the larger goal of winning the series.

Slate nods. "If we do well, he'd like to pick up more league races. The entire team needs to be in agreement. It means travel, and a lot more work."

"Yes! I mean, of course." I close off the flurry of

words and glance at Gabe. He's looking around the garage, and his rich kid comments come back all too clear. Will he walk off like last time?

Slate's watching him too, so I hold my breath. Gabe's dark eyes glance around the room, then land on mine. I search for that spark of hatred. Maybe that isn't what he felt. After seeing his home, it's possible it was just wounded pride and longing all mixed into a sour elixir.

He sighs. "I'm in."

I wish I could leap into the sky. A league race!

"Great," Slate says, still looking around. "I'll be right back."

Gabe and I stand in uneasy silence. His frantic efforts to pull me from the quicksand ease my tension a little. I grimace as I limp toward the wall, but trying to cover it doesn't do much good. It's wounded pride that makes me hate limping so much. It helps me understand Gabe even more. I hit the garage door opener and then wince.

The wide door clacks as it rolls up, revealing the yard and the river beyond.

Gabe strides forward, taking in the view. He crosses his arms, the fresh, salty air wafting over us. "What you did yesterday . . ."

As he struggles with the words, I turn toward him. Our past at school is as strong as the tide and just as relentless.

He looks me in the eye. "Thank you."

I nod, knowing I've got to swim against that riptide too. "Anybody would've done it." I pause, hoping I don't ruin everything. "You know, I'm not better than you because of all this." I sweep one arm around the garage.

That spark flashes in his eye. "Yeah, right."

"Listen, you and I, we're equals in my book. And on Team Taylor, you're indispensable. We'll never get to a track without you." I know how true it is.

Gabe looks at me, his shoulders relaxing.

Slate bursts through the door. "New plan, boys. We're moving the shop here. Then I won't have to play bus driver, and we'll get more work done. Logan, your mom said it's fine. Your parents are okay with widening the driveway for the semi to fit."

Moving the shop to Burnout Bay? If my legs weren't so sore, I'd be leaping up and down! But then I glance at Gabe, knowing that being there will rub him the wrong way.

He's frowning, staring out at the water. Without yesterday, he'd probably be long gone.

"Sounds great," I venture as if the words are no big deal, but inside I can't believe 77 will be right in my garage!

Gabe sighs. "It'll be easier to get to, I guess."

I clamp my mouth shut, knowing how easy it would be to ruin our truce.

"I have a lot of work to do," Slate says. "Gabe, I'll drop you at home, so I can get started."

Within minutes, I'm alone again in the garage that will soon be full of cars. I can't stop grinning. I ease down to the floor again, the excitement washing away the exhaustion in my muscles.

The door opens again. Piper is standing there with Mom. Wincing, I scramble to my feet, regretting the hasty movement. "Hey," I say, stifling a groan. "Piper."

She gives me a shy wave. Mom looks at us with a sparkle in her eye. "I'll be in the kitchen if you need me."

All I see is Piper's face when Gabe, Slate, and I were smashed together inside Sophia. Words scramble up inside my head as I stare at her.

"Your mom told me what happened yesterday. Are you okay?"

I'm so relieved that she bypassed seeing me sitting in Gabe's lap that I laugh. "Oh that, yeah, I'll be fine."

I take a step and then crumple forward, proving myself wrong. Piper's there, supporting my elbow. "Maybe we can sit down?"

"Sounds good." I ease down to the garage steps. "Thanks for checking on me. Oh, I forgot! I have something for you."

"You do?" she asks, her eyes sparkling.

"Yeah, but it feels like it's a million miles away."

"Where is it?" she asks, wrinkling her nose.

"Over there, in that toolbox." I hold out my hand.

"Ah, so your legs are worse than you're letting on."

I shrug, "it's in the top drawer."

She gets up and pulls it open. "Oh, a socket set. Just what I always wanted."

I roll my eyes in response to her teasing tone. "Behind that."

She pulls out a pair of new Bones Super Reds skateboard bearings and hot-pink wheels, then goes still. She stands there so long that nerves settle in. Did I go too far?

She turns to me, the breeze from the open bay doors blowing her hair over one shoulder.

I clear my throat. "You helped me reach the

goal I wanted most, keeping up my grades so I could race. I thought it was time somebody helped you reach yours."

She fingers the new wheels and bearings, looking down. I wish I could read her thoughts. Then her eyes meet mine. "Logan Reed, that's one of the nicest things anyone's ever done for me. But I'm not very good at skateboarding."

"Maybe not yet. But you will be."

She smiles. "Thank you." Then her nose wrinkles up on one side, "Logan, I have to ask, what *were* you doing sitting in Gabe's lap?"

- 18 -

Five days later, we're loading everything into the semi. My nerves are on fire, but it's not just me who's nervous. Gabe and Slate feel it too. The ECMD 150 is the longest race I've ever competed in. I rub sweat off my palms as Slate maneuvers the trailer on the throughway. The drive is too short to calm my nerves.

At least my legs have recovered, and I can walk without pain.

Slate pulls in, and we stare at the track. At just over half a mile long, North Wilkesboro Speedway seems huge. Slate points to the turns. "You've got a thirteen percent bank on these turns. If you don't use it, there's no way you can stay with the pack."

I lay my right hand over my stomach. "Thanks Slate. If I wasn't nervous before, I am now."

He grimaces. "Sorry. This is a big day for us. Our focus is on learning and identifying areas for improvement. We'll give it our best and, win or lose, Team Taylor will come out better for it. Safety first today, okay, boys?"

We nod, staring at the pits.

Gabe blinks rapidly. "Thirteen percent bank. I have to change the camber."

I nod. 77 isn't set up for this track, and changing the angle of the wheels will make the car able to make those turns.

Slate signs the paperwork that a lady hands through the door and then claps his hands, making us jump. "Load up, boys. We've got our work cut out for us."

In the massive pits, our rig looks average instead of overbearing like it does at the smaller tracks. We're in the big leagues now, and a nagging voice tells me I'm not ready.

Another team is unloading their trailer with a fancy ramp that reaches high, where the cars are stored on a second level. Gabe presses his nose against the window, staring. I guess we're both feeling our age, or the lack of it.

When we push 77 down the ramp, a solid feeling fills me. Slate pulls out his ever-present clipboard. "Okay, boys, we've got one hundred and fifty laps. That's ninety miles of racing. Everything on the car has to be tight, clean, and perfect."

I squat down, holding onto the doughnut I ate for breakfast by sheer willpower. Slowing my breath helps the green feeling. *Maybe doughnuts weren't the best choice before a big race.*

"Ah . . . " Gabe's sigh doesn't make me feel better. "I'm gonna need some help."

We spend the next hour with the three of us squeezed under 77, adjusting the camber to fit the track.

Serious race teams from all over the country fill the pits, all of them seasoned competitors. That does nothing to settle my nerves.

"Okay, that's it," Gabe says. "I think."

"*You think?*" I ask. "Are you sure?" Doing 160 mph on a mechanic's "I think" isn't cool.

"Yeah, I'm sure," he says with a smirk, "I was just messing with you, hombre. I reviewed these specs with my uncle this morning. You're good to go."

I shake out the tingling in my fingertips. Slate's

legs appear as he strides around the car, so I roll out from beneath 77.

"We have five practice laps, then the track inspector will be here."

I look at the grandstands. It's so intimidating yet so alluring. A grin spreads across my face. Getting on the asphalt will fix everything.

In a few seconds, I'm in my new race gear, feeling more at home and trying to hold back a nervous giggle. These laps won't count for anything; they're just for fun. *Pure fun.*

I barely touch 77 as I hop in feet first. Slate's there, leaning on the sill.

As the seat hugs my body, a thought strikes me. *I'm the guy in the car!* For a second, the thought grips me so hard I can't hold back an amazed sigh.

"You alright?" Slate asks, his right eye tight.

"Being in here feels better."

He points to the turn straight ahead. "Go easy for the first two laps. On a track like this, you need to prep the car. Before making the turn, give the wheel the slightest bump, so that the car is ready."

"Okay." I say, not getting what he means at all. "I'll try it."

Slate slaps the roof, and I put the car into gear.

77 surges forward, making my skin tingle as I recall the wild chase through the woods. This should be easy.

By turn two I'm at top short-track speeds, which I've been comfortable at for a long time. As I approach 150 mph, my heart pounds. The straightaway zips past, and I enter turn three.

77 shimmies, the intense speed making the wheels feel too light, and the far wall approaches way too fast! I shout, wrenching the wheel.

The tires slide sideways as the concrete wall looms closer! As I fight the wild slide, the wheels finally find a grip. I fishtail out of the turn, my senses on fire and every nerve tingling.

"Okay," I say to 77's screaming engine, "let's try that again." I'm back on turn one in seconds, so I try to prep the car. I turn the wheel just a hair, but it throws me off the racing line! It isn't any prettier than turn three.

By lap four, my stress level is through the roof. What if Slate pulls me from this race? Hearing him say I'm not ready would be . . . I can't even think of it. Maybe he'd be right.

But it's no use putting it off, so I brake as I enter our slim area in the pits.

"Slide over, kid," Slate says.

That's impossible in a race car because of the roll bars that run between the seats. So, I pull myself out and walk around, my heart sinking. I slide into the passenger seat and look over at Slate. It's the first time I've ever seen him wearing a helmet. Judging by the look he gives me, my mouth must be hanging open.

"What? You think I only drive on roads?"

I stare at the track. This seat isn't nearly as comfortable as mine.

Slate's muscular frame is a super-tight fit, but he lets out a long sigh after he snaps on the steering wheel and buckles into the five-point harness. "That feels good. It's been a while."

The deep satisfaction in his voice raises a million questions, but he pushes the start button, and speaking becomes pointless over the engine's roar.

He clutches, and we take off. I relax against the seat. This is weird. Really weird!

Slate's doing 100 mph long before turn one. Something tells me he's done this before. It takes a full lap to reach top speed. We must be doing over 160 mph! 77 sticks to the pavement like glue due to the bank of the turns. It's nothing like when I drove.

With every lap, Slate gains more speed, and 77 responds with perfect control. When he pulls into the pits, I'm shell shocked, limp in the seat. The questions can't escape fast enough into the sudden silence after he shuts 77 down.

"Why aren't you the driver for Team Taylor? Why didn't I know you could drive?"

"Take it easy, kid. Man! That felt good." Slate rubs the dash as if it's made of gold.

– 19 –

Slate sighs, still rubbing the steering wheel. I stare at him in awe, my respect for him ratcheting higher.

"Racing was my only dream," he says, his voice soft.

"Why did you stop?" I ask as I pull off my helmet.

"Had no choice. I wrecked the first time I drove at Daytona. Had some nerve damage that messed with my eyes. I can't pass the vision exam for my racing license anymore."

Hot tears prick my eyes. *He lost everything that day.* The sensation is all too familiar after waiting to hear about my license.

He shrugs. "Those who can't do . . . teach." He shrugs. "I couldn't walk away from racing altogether. Being a crew chief keeps me in the pulse of the game. It's a pretty good gig, depending on the driver."

His gaze is so intense that my stomach does a flip.

Then he laughs, reaching over to ruffle my hair. "Remember, we aren't here to win today. We're here to learn the ropes."

I nod, feeling like a ten-year-old in college.

"The car's tight," he says.

What he doesn't say is plain: that near spinout was all me.

"Sorry." I feel pressure from all sides. At home, I have to bump up my grades even higher, something I once thought impossible. Now I'm facing skills I thought I had but don't.

"I'm not sorry. Every driver has to grow, and that's okay. Expect some rear wheel drift when taking turns at high speeds. Maybe not enough to see, but you'll feel it. You've got to ride that sensation hard. The feel for it will come. It won't take you long to recognize the safe zone. Loosen up, and trust the car. Keep every movement as smooth as glass. And don't forget to enjoy it."

Soon, I'm back in the driver's seat, with 77's roar filling my soul. "Let's go, boy."

I pull out, forcing my arms to stay loose. Turn one is easy since I'm only doing 100 mph. I pay attention to the steep tilt of the track. At full speed, it felt as flat as a pancake.

"Trust the car . . . " I speed up by 10 mph each lap, easing into the place deep inside where every cell is focused.

A glance shows the speedo's readout: 162. I nod, jamming down the shot of nerves. *As smooth as glass.*

I pull in, a grin spreading until I can't hold in a whoop.

The day flies past with inspections, paperwork, and last-minute tweaks to 77.

Gabe and I work shoulder to shoulder. "Okay, we need a final check on tire pressures," he says. "Both left tires require twenty-eight psi while the front right needs fifty-two psi, and the rear needs fifty psi."

I nod as if I knew that. I have to admit, competing here would've been impossible without Gabe's knowledge and skill.

"Sure thing, boss," I say, earning a shocked expression from Gabe.

Like a hummingbird, Slate is there one second and

gone the next, hustling to get the paperwork straight.

"Well, boys, what do you think?" a voice says as we finish the tires.

"John!" I stand up, smiling.

"This is a dream come true," he says, rubbing 77's hood.

I shake out my hands, knowing how much is riding on my shoulders.

He smiles. "Logan, today I want you to just take everything in. There's no pressure to win. I mean that. Winning for us tonight looks like a clean finish and ice cream afterwards."

"Thanks, John," I say, knowing I might have imploded from the pressure otherwise.

Hand in hand, Mom and Dad approach.

"Logan!" Mom cries, but I cut her off.

"Don't tell me to be careful!"

She laughs. "Okay, I'll just say it in my head."

Dad's hand rests on my shoulder. "Your commitment and effort, particularly in school, means a lot to us."

I can't seem to find my voice as his words strike deep.

"It's time!" Slate says as he strides up. "Logan, you'll need at least one pit stop for tires and fuel."

I nod. *A race long enough to need a pit stop.* I release a slow breath.

"I'll radio you when to pull in. One hundred and fifty laps—Gabe, is the car ready?"

"Yes, sir!" His confident answer soothes my nerves.

I pull my helmet on and step forward. Gabe holds me back with a grip on my forearm.

"Hey, you'll do great."

Time seems to lurch to a halt as I look him in the eye. All our past blows away like rust under a sandblaster. I slap his shoulder. "That's because you got 77 ready."

He grunts, one side of his mouth tipping up. "Drive like at the airstrip, and you'll have this win in the bag."

"Um . . . I totaled that car."

He frowns, scratching his chin. "Good point. Then minus the totaling part."

I laugh, shaking my head as I hop into 77. I push the start button and grip the wheel. A glance out the window fills me to the brim. The five people standing there are my team, *my family.*

I shift into first. *This race is for them.*

– 20 –

The pace car veers off, but instead of the normal elated feeling, I grimace, searching for a good spot in the pack.

We surge forward, and it's clear the other drivers are at home there. I'm the new guy, just trying to trust the car.

We sweep into turn one, and I hold the center position. *Only 599 more turns to go.* That was a bad thought, but one thing's for sure: I'll be comfortable doing it by then . . . or I'll be dead.

I slam the steering wheel. "Come on, Logan!"

I know Slate can hear me through the radio, and the shot of embarrassment shakes me out of the downward spiral of my thoughts.

By turn four, drivers are jockeying for position. I grimace as I watch three cars pull ahead. I've always been in that pack, among the leaders who dominate the race.

A clean race is all John wants, and that's what I intend to give him. Of course, it wouldn't hurt to nab a second-place finish . . .

"How's your fuel pressure?" Slate's voice in my helmet radio reminds me it could've been him out there. Maybe a clean race is the most important thing.

"Fifty-eight," I report, drafting behind a red car. I hug the inside, using the draft to slingshot around turn two.

"Nice move," Slate says.

Laps sweep by, and with each one, I trust the car a little more, inching forward. But a caution flag snaps overhead, and we ease off, every driver searching for the issue.

A blue car sits sideways in turn three.

"Pit stop, Logan. Let's use that caution flag!"

I pull in right behind the lead car. His pit crew leaps the concrete barrier in unison. They're like an army, seven guys diving straight to their specific jobs. I count off seconds as they work. They finish a complete tire change and refuel in fourteen seconds.

The leader burns rubber, zipping back onto the track as Slate and Gabe move to my third tire.

"We're going to need to work on pit stop times!" I say. The caution flag switches to green, but 77 is still jacked up!

Slate growls, slamming the final fresh tire home. The *zzrip, zzrip, zzrip* of Gabe's lug gun sends shots of adrenaline up my spine. 77 slams flat as they release the jack.

"Go!" Slate shouts, convincing me he wants to win as much as I do.

I shift hard, clutching in quick succession. The field's a mess after the caution. It's super tough to tell what position I'm in. But it doesn't really matter. There's only one that I want—first.

I was light-footing it out there before. But now, with only twenty laps left, I let my usual edge of aggressive driving take over.

I surge past two cars on turn four, then someone bumps my rear fender.

Everything is chaos for a second as my reflexes take over, fighting the fishtail.

"Whoo! Nice recovery!" Slate's praise helps my heart slow to a normal pace.

I grit my teeth as the two cars I just passed zip

by. "Come on!"

"Take it easy, Logan. There are plenty more races to come!"

But I can't leave it at that. As the laps count down, I edge closer to the three leaders. They're far out ahead now, and I force down a feeling of hopelessness.

With five laps left, I fight gravity and inertia around the turns. A complete spinout is only a hair's breadth away.

Then, with two laps remaining, there's only an empty track between me and the leaders. John's words to Bobby long ago make me cringe. I don't want fourth-place finishes forever.

I hate to deliver one tonight, but I can't catch them. I flash under the checkered flag all by myself, in the open space between the winners and losers.

Exhaustion hits me as I exit the course. Racing for that long has taken an enormous amount of energy.

Slate's there, his massive arms pulling me out of 77's window. He crushes me in a hug and then I ping-pong from Mom and Dad to John, my legs like rubber.

They're all shouting as if I won.

"Nice finish!" John claps Slate on the back. Dad

lets me go, and Gabe's standing there.

"Don't you dare hug me," I say with a laugh.

He punches me in the shoulder. "Wouldn't dream of it, man."

"Watch out, NASCAR!" John shouts. "Team Taylor is coming for you!"

I snort. "We've got a long way to go."

But their excitement is contagious as I run one hand over 77's gleaming hood.

— EPILOGUE —

Burnout Bay is perfect, with 77 and 22 tucked in the center doors. The salty breeze swirls, and the reeds rustle. Bigger tracks are just like those reeds. At first they seemed to hide untold dangers. But after being in the mud flats, they seem so safe and familiar.

Slate rubs his chin, muttering. He's been poring over stats for the last two days. "The pits took way too long. We need a bigger team, somebody with fast hands."

I don't respond, knowing he's happy in his own bubble.

Footsteps scrape the concrete. Gabe strides up, wearing a jumpsuit. That means he'll be touching up the paint where I got shoved during the race.

Something is tucked under his arm. Without a word, he picks up a hammer and ladder, moving to the rear wall of the garage. I weave my head, trying to see what he's doing. Then he steps back, revealing a picture frame. Inside it, the wrench of peace is mounted above the following words: "The future's on fire."

Gabe nods at me, then starts sanding 77's fender. I turn, staring out over the White Oak River. I'm finally *home*.

Other Bakken Books Stories

Camping books for kids

Mystery books for kids

Hunting books for kids

Fishing books for kids

www.bakkenbooks.com

Math adventures for kids

History adventures for kids

Space adventures for kids

Humorous adventures for kids